# SWORD ART ONLINE PROGRESSIVE

## VOLUME 5

Reki Kawahara

abec

bee-pee

YEN ON

NEW YORK

SWORD ART ONLINE PROGRESSIVE Volume 5
REKI KAWAHARA

Translation by Stephen Paul
Cover art by abec

SWORD ART ONLINE PROGRESSIVE Volume 5
© REKI KAWAHARA 2018
First published in Japan in 2018 by KADOKAWA CORPORATION, Tokyo.
English translation rights arranged with KADOKAWA CORPORATION, Tokyo, through Tuttle-Mori Agency, Inc., Tokyo.

English translation © 2018 by Yen Press, LLC

Yen On
1290 Avenue of the Americas
New York, NY 10104

Visit us at yenpress.com
facebook.com/yenpress
twitter.com/yenpress
yenpress.tumblr.com
instagram.com/yenpress

First Yen On Edition: November 2018

Yen On is an imprint of Yen Press, LLC.
The Yen On name and logo are trademarks of Yen Press, LLC.

Library of Congress Cataloging-in-Publication Data

Names: Kawahara, Reki, author. | Paul, Stephen (Translator), translator.
Title: Sword art online progressive / Reki Kawahara; translation by Stephen Paul.
Description: First Yen On edition. | New York, NY : Yen On, 2016–
Identifiers: LCCN 2016029472 | ISBN 9780316259361 (v. 1 : pbk) |
  ISBN 9780316342179 (v. 2 : pbk) | ISBN 9780316348836 (v. 3 : pbk) |
  ISBN 9780316545426 (v. 4 : pbk) | ISBN 9781975328146 (v. 5 : pbk)
Subjects: | CYAC: Virtual reality—Fiction. | Science fiction.
Classification: LCC PZ7.K1755 Swr 2016 | DDC [Fic]—dc23
LC record available at https://lccn.loc.gov/2016029472

ISBNs: 978-1-9753-2814-6 (paperback)
        978-1-9753-8311-4 (ebook)

10 9 8 7 6 5 4 3 2 1

LSC-C

Printed in the United States of America

# "THIS MIGHT BE A GAME, BUT IT'S NOT SOMETHING YOU PLAY."

—Akihiko Kayaba, *Sword Art Online* programmer

# SWORD ART ONLINE
## PROGRESSIVE

*CANON OF THE GOLDEN RULE (START)*

SIXTH FLOOR OF AINCRAD, JANUARY 2023

*"PAH-CHOO!"*

I spun around to ascertain the nature of the odd sound behind my back.

The fencer who was my temporary partner had her hands over her nose. A few seconds later, she arched her back and loosed another *"Pah-choo!"*

"…Was that a sneeze, or are you saying you want patchouli for your bath tonight?" I quipped, earning myself a glare.

"I don't like patchouli."

"What about pumpkin spice?"

"Nope."

"Maybe parsnip?"

"Nope…Hey, that's not even a thing!" she snapped, bringing the joke full circle. Asuna, the level-18 swordswoman, sighed. "It was a sneeze…I think. I'm not sure."

"Huh? Wh-what does that mean? Shouldn't you be able to tell if you sneezed or not…?" I wondered, seriously this time. I came to a stop in the middle of the path.

Just an hour or two ago, the central street of Karluin, the main town of the fifth floor of Aincrad, had been packed with people, but now it was completely empty. The countdown party with fireworks to celebrate the arrival of the year 2023 was over, and the players had cleared out, returning to their inn rooms—or back to the wilderness to hunt.

Asuna and I watched the fireworks from the old castle ruins outside town and waited for the area to grow quiet before we left. This was because we'd had a dangerous, unexpected encounter in the ruins. Even with my excellent Search skill, it would be harder to detect someone trailing us in a crowd.

I casually checked behind me as I waited for Asuna to reply. To my surprise, she had a very rational response: "Sneezes are involuntary bodily functions designed to either raise your body temperature when it's cold or expel a foreign object from the nasal cavity, right? Neither are necessary for a player avatar to do."

"Oh. Well, I guess…that's a good point…"

"So if the *SAO* system is artificially reproducing some kind of sneezing function, I'm not certain that can be called a 'real' sneeze…That's my point."

"I see…" I murmured, impressed. Then my own nose started to tickle. It was either the chill or the repetition of the word *sneeze* that was making me conscious of it. Eventually, I couldn't hold it any longer.

"*Broosh!*" I exploded.

Asuna grinned smugly at me. "What's that? Are you saying you want bruschetta for breakfast tomorrow?"

"…What's bruschetta?"

"It's a kind of Italian finger food."

"That actually sounds kind of good," I murmured, imagining what this bruschetta might look like and unconsciously tugging the collar of my coat tighter before I realized what I was doing. "Hey… is it just me or is it kinda cold here?"

"…Yes, it's rather chilly…"

Asuna wore a hooded wool cape, but it was over a miniskirt that didn't seem to defend much against the elements. A man who was smooth and considerate would put his own coat on her without saying a word, but as a loser gamer and shut-in, I wasn't equipped with any skills that I couldn't earn in a video game.

Fortunately, before I said or did anything to embarrass myself, Asuna opened her menu and adjusted her equipment mannequin. Light covered the pale legs exposed by her leather battle skirt, then faded into white tights.

There shouldn't be any artificial fibers in this world, given the setting, but somehow, the skintight material seemed to shine in the light—I couldn't help but stare. Before, she would've retaliated with a cold look, sharp words, and perhaps even some kind of physical attack—but this time, Asuna just cleared her throat and looked up at the bottom of the floor above, visible in the dark.

"…Well, it is the beginning of the year, so you would expect it to be cold…and yet, the fourth floor was quite warm when we were down there recently. How does Aincrad handle the seasons of the year?"

"Um…it was August in the beta test, but even though the sun felt hot at midday, it wasn't, like, unpleasantly hot. And it was nothing like the suffocating muggy heat of midsummer in real life."

"Hmm…I suppose if it were really that hot, nobody would be able to bother with full plate armor and the like."

"Good point. Makes me wonder what those old European knights did during the summer…"

"The Knights Templar of the Kingdom of Jerusalem lost to Saladin's forces because the heat sapped their strength."

"Ah…I see."

As usual, Asuna had plenty of facts to back herself up. I started getting the nasty feeling that she might eventually learn more about Aincrad than even I knew, so I quickly brought us back to the matter at hand:

"The point is…Aincrad does model the seasons to an extent, but I don't think it actually simulates heat and cold to a level that is uncomfortable. I mean, this isn't nearly as bad as the midwinter weather we'd be feeling in the real world, right?"

"Even dressed like this, the worst it does is make me sneeze."

"But there are exceptions. I seem to remember reading about floors that are winter or summer all year round...according to a magazine article or something..."

"Hmm..."

Asuna glanced up once more, then wondered, "You didn't find this floor of eternal summer during the beta test?"

"Well, it *was* summer at the time...but I do remember a beach on the south side of floor seven. It had white sand, coconut trees, and a bunch of players enjoying their summer vacation in swimsuits."

"The way you say that makes me assume you didn't take part," she noted insightfully.

"Well, a guy celebrating his vacation all alone is kinda sad, right?" I admitted. "It's fine. I was focused on getting through the game."

This desperate excuse made Asuna grin enough to forget the cold. She patted me on the back. "South side of the seventh floor? I'll remember that. If it really is an area of eternal summer..."

"...Then?"

"Mmm. I think I'll keep it under wraps until then. Let's get going to the next main town. The sixth floor starts in earnest tomorrow...er, today."

The fencer walked off at a brisk pace, and I had to rush to catch up, feeling skeptical. It had been more than a month since our temporary partnership began, and I still couldn't tell what she was thinking most of the time.

*But I guess that's part of her charm*, I thought, which was uncharacteristic of me. I shook my head, and my nostrils began itching again. It was harmless enough in the safety of town, but if I sneezed in a dungeon while trying to hide, the consequences could be disastrous. I'd have to study how to suppress the urge.

I tried holding my nose, then my breath, but neither worked. Eventually, my itchiness meter reached its peak.

"*Vah-kesh!*"

Asuna stopped and turned around to look at me with a 60 percent annoyed glare and 40 percent enigmatic smile.

"Are you that excited about summer vacation?" she asked.

"N-no, I..."

"Then we'd better get through the sixth floor as quickly as we can."

"I'm telling you, it's not like that!"

But no matter how much I protested, the smirk never left the fencer's face. In the end, I wasn't even sure if I really wanted the seventh floor to be an everlasting summer paradise or not.

# 1

EVEN ON THE OTHER SIDE OF THE TELEPORT GATE, the air was still chilly.

Unlike Karluin, the fifth floor's main town that existed in the ruins of an ancient city, Stachion was a pristinely built town on the sixth floor. The main material of construction was a shiny gray rock like polished granite, and every single structure was made of blocks exactly the same size in a grid pattern, about eight inches to a side—meaning that everything was straight lines and angles. The effect was so striking that when I first visited this place in the beta test, my reaction was—well, exactly the same as Asuna's now:

"Ooh…It's so blocky…"

"Well, we *are* trapped in a video game," I replied, the standard joke in Stachion. It earned me a piercing, cold glare that lowered my body temperature even further.

I tugged the collar of my coat up, but it did nothing to keep the chill away. It was still much better than actual winter, but one of the more annoying parts of the virtual world was that once you noticed it was warm or cold, the only way to *stop* feeling it required some kind of in-game logic.

It was three o'clock in the morning, January 1, 2023.

The frontline population's New Year's enthusiasm had burned itself out with the fireworks show, and hardly a soul could be found in the teleport gate square of Stachion. A dry north wind blew through the empty space, which was about fifty yards to a side. I figured it would be cold for Asuna and her miniskirt, but between the fleece-lined cape and tights, she seemed to be protected enough.

*Or perhaps the chill I'm feeling now is more than just the NerveGear's artificial sensations...*

In the old castle ruins to the east of Karluin, where Asuna and I were going to watch the fireworks show, I'd left to get food and run straight into an attack by a mysterious figure in a black poncho. The castle was within the protective limits of the town, of course, so his plan had been to cleverly trick me into thinking I was still inside the anti-criminal code zone while he lured me into the castle's basement, which was actually *outside* the safe area.

The man in the black poncho had snuck up right behind me, despite my proficiency in the Search skill, pointed a knife to my back, and whispered, "It's showtime." The coldness of that voice would not leave my ears...The way it richly lilted as though in song—and yet alien in how it betrayed no discernable emotion.

I was nearly too late to detect his bluff. I rattled off a series of sword skills within the safe zone, hoping to push him into a simulated stunned state, but he used an unfamiliar smoke screen item to escape. I rushed back to the room where I'd left Asuna and was so relieved to see my temporary partner safe that I hugged her—earning me a vicious hook to the right flank. But that hadn't solved the underlying problem.

My guess was that the man in the black poncho was the boss of Morte, the axman who had tried to kill me in a duel. The leader of the PK group agitators who had tempted the Legend Braves into their equipment-upgrading scam and who'd tried to get the Dragon Knights Brigade (DKB) and Aincrad Liberation Squad (ALS) to go to war against each other.

Thanks to me and Asuna intervening, neither of those incidents developed into disaster. That was why the man in the black poncho came to eliminate me directly, I assumed—but they weren't going to give up from a single failed attempt. I'd have to watch out for danger at all times from now on.

And there was one even larger problem:

There was a high possibility that they'd go after Asuna, too. That, above all else, I had to prevent, and yet, I still hadn't told her about the attack I'd just suffered.

I wasn't going to keep it a secret, of course. By tonight's inn stay at the latest, I'd tell her all about the man in detail and give her another primer on the basic tenets of PvP combat. But all I could grapple with at the moment was what had happened right after we ascended to the fifth floor.

It was Asuna who'd asked for a lesson in player-versus-player battle—whether you called it PvP or dueling or whatever. After the fight against Morte on the fourth floor, I immediately recognized the importance of this lesson, so in an empty corner of the ruins, we engaged in a proper duel.

But once we actually faced each other with swords up, she couldn't move. Instead, she tearfully lowered her blade and said she didn't want to do it.

It wasn't that she had no talent for PvP. When one of the PKers had nearly taken her Chivalric Rapier in the ruins dungeon of the fifth floor, the way she utilized a looting monster to get it back was brilliant work. Once that imagination of hers had both knowledge and experience to bolster it, she'd be able to put her already considerable talent to use in the arena of man-to-man combat.

But under the current rules of *SAO*, where dying in-game meant dying in real life, a player duel was therefore a fight to the death. If both sides were evenly matched, the winner would be whoever had less hesitation about taking the other's life. Or in other words, without that level of cruelty, any potential victory in a close fight was likely to result in a loss.

If I was going to teach Asuna how to fight another player, it was more important that she learned that cold rationality than any fiddly mechanical techniques I might teach her. I'd never killed another player myself, of course, but if it was necessary to protect myself or my partner, I believed I could do it. Or phrased another way, I wasn't a good enough person at heart to hesitate in the heat of the moment.

But Asuna was different. She was much more kindhearted than me—with an upright and honest soul. I didn't want to tell her that she should be cold and cruel and ready to kill…

"…Hey, Kirito." I looked up and saw my partner right in front of me, concerned. "Why did you clam up all of a sudden? You aren't hungry already, are you?"

"N-no, that's not it…"

"Then can I ask my first question of the sixth floor?"

"G-go right ahead," I prompted. We'd been in the middle of the tenth floor when the beta test ended, so including this floor, there were only four and a half left where I could actually answer Asuna's questions. *After all that's happened, we're already on the sixth floor*, I marveled.

Then the fencer asked simply, "What's this?"

"Eh?"

Asuna pointed down at our feet. I followed her slender index finger to one of the gray tiles that paved the teleport square. Like the blocks that made up the buildings, it was just ordinary stone about eight inches to a side, but one in every four or so tiles had an Arabic numeral from one to nine on it.

"Ahh…yes, these…" I took two steps back and pointed down, just like she did. "See how the line between them is thicker here?"

"You're right…"

"This thicker line is where the tiles are split into nine-by-nine grids of eighty-one tiles total. Does this look familiar to you?"

"Nine by nine…" Asuna mumbled. She blinked three times, then looked up and grinned. "Ohhh, I get it. This is a sudoku puzzle! I was pretty good at them. Interesting, so the tiles of the square make a puzz…le…"

She trailed off as she got another look around the teleport

square. If you ignored the actual teleport gate in the middle, the entire square, fifty yards to a side, was covered in these tiles. And those sudoku puzzles with their number hints ran from end to end.

"…How many of these puzzles are there?"

"If it hasn't changed from the beta, there are twenty-seven rows and columns of these eighty-one-tile sets. Since the exact middle one is taken up by the gate, that means it's twenty-seven squared, minus one. Which equals seven hundred twenty-eight."

"Seven hun—" Asuna gasped quietly. She looked away from the numbers at her feet. "For a moment, I was interested in solving them all. I am no longer interested."

"A wise decision," I said with a sage tone channeling that of any given village elder NPC. "During the beta test, those youngsters who fell prey to the lures of sudoku and gave up on helping us advance the game were called sudokers out of respect…"

"That's an even sadder nickname than the 'hoarders' who got addicted to finding coins in the ruins. But given how many of these puzzles there are, does that mean there's some mammoth reward if you solve them all?"

"You'd think so," I said, normally this time. "I was under that assumption during the beta, and the sudokers certainly believed it. But the nasty part about this is…all the hint numbers get switched up at midnight every night."

"*What?!* So you're saying…if you wanted to solve the whole batch, you'd have to do seven hundred twenty-eight sudoku puzzles in a span of twenty-four hours?" Asuna exclaimed. She started counting with her fingers. "Let's see…At a glance, these look like maximum difficulty, so even an expert would take a good twenty minutes to solve one. Multiplying that by seven hundred twenty-eight would be fourteen thousand five hundred sixty minutes…divided by sixty makes two hundred forty-two hours and forty minutes…"

I had to admit that the speed of this calculation backed up her claim to be "pretty good" at math puzzles.

"That's over ten days!" she exclaimed, her shock turning to annoyance. "That's impossible! I'm not going to do them!"

"N-nobody said you had to...At any rate, the sudokers split up as a group to try to tackle them, and even then, they weren't fast enough to beat it by midnight. So on the last day of the beta, they resorted to forbidden measures."

"Forbidden...?"

"Since you could log in or out as much as you wanted in the beta, they would memorize the placement of the hints, then log out and use an external program to solve the problem..."

"Oh, I see," Asuna said, smirking.

I concluded the heroes' tale. "They beat the whole lot just an hour before the end of the test. Now, do you see how just one tile out of the eighty-one is a darker color?"

"Hmm, you're right."

"The numbers in those tiles are some kind of key. So at the end of all that work, the sudokers got seven hundred twenty-eight key numbers..."

"Uh-huh?"

"And that was it."

"Huh?"

"Nobody knew what to do with them. They say that for the last hour until the end of the test, the tragic sudokers were reduced to running around the square in their underpants, screaming the numbers and going mad."

"..."

Asuna's annoyance turned to pity. She gazed out at the wide space of flat stone and numbers, lonely in the moonlight. Without another word on the matter, she closed her eyes for a moment, then waved her right hand to bring up the menu.

"Oh my, it's past three. We should go to the inn already. I assume the DKB and ALS will be sleeping in, too, but I'd still like to get up and back to business by ten o'clock."

"Good idea," I agreed, reminded of my earlier anxiety. But Asuna's smile was earnest and innocent.

"Here's question two, then. What's your recommended place to stay in Stachion?"

For about three minutes, we walked east down a road paved with the same tiles as the square, until I led Asuna to a nondescript, midsize inn—though, given the way everything in the town was built out of the same little blocks, it was hard for any of them to acquire distinguishing features.

I pushed open the wooden door (at least that was different) and checked in at the counter, reserving two adjacent rooms on the second floor. The empty hallway up there turned out to be ten blocks wide, just over six feet, with no place to hide.

I'd kept my hackles up from the moment we'd arrived at this level of Aincrad till we got to this inn, but no one had been following or watching us—at least, so I thought. But I couldn't be absolutely certain, because now that I suspected the man in the black poncho had a Hiding skill at least as good as my Search, I could no longer trust my eyes and ears.

I walked to the end of the hallway, keenly aware of the stress of being in potential danger. Asuna was in Room 201 in the corner, while I was in 202 just before it.

The fencer yawned gracefully in front of her door and glanced at me. "Um...shall we meet in the restaurant downstairs at eight...or, no, nine o'clock?"

"That's fine with me."

"Then good night, Kirito."

She waved and grabbed the door handle. But the handle rattled in place and resisted her pressure.

"Wh...whoops? Is the other one my room...?" she wondered, shuffling over with sleepy eyes. I grabbed her shoulders.

"Nope, you had the right one."

"Uh...why isn't it opening, then?"

Her question was a reasonable one. Inn rooms in Aincrad didn't have keys as a general rule; doors automatically unlocked for the owner (or their registered friends and party members)—a system choice made for player convenience. And we were in a party together, so even if she'd gotten my room, the door should have opened.

I walked over to Asuna, who was half sleepy and half skeptical, and pointed at the 201 attached to her door. On closer look, the square plate was split into a four-by-four grid, with the other squares having fainter numbers of their own and a single blank space in the bottom right corner.

"Doesn't this look familiar, too?" I prompted.

Asuna blinked about five times and finally said, "Oh…is this a fifteen puzzle…?"

"Bingo. Only in this case, the numbers go from zero to fourteen."

"……Are you saying that if I don't solve this puzzle, the door won't open?"

"Correct."

"………"

Now her expression was 20 percent sleepiness, 20 percent suspicion, and 60 percent disgust. I hastily added, "B-but don't worry. There's a trick to this…"

I reached up to the plate and started sliding the wooden numbers around, which were randomly placed aside from the Room 201 numbers.

"See, it's easy to get zero through seven in the top two rows, right? After that, you just line up the eight and twelve in the lower left, then put the nine and thirteen next to them, and the rest is natural…"

The moment I slid the fourteen into the right spot, there was an audible click as the door unlocked. Then I pushed down the handle, and the door opened inward this time.

"…Thank you," Asuna said, but her expression did not suggest gratitude. I'd brought her to this inn for a reason—of all the puzzle doors in Stachion, the ones here were on the simple side.

But there was something more important to explain to her now—more important than the facts of this town or this entire floor. Asuna was quite exhausted, and I was reaching the peak of my fatigue, too, but the last thing I wanted to do now was put off this decision until tomorrow, only to regret it.

"Well, good night..." Asuna started to vanish through the doorway.

I raised my voice just 5 percent higher than normal. "Asuna!"

"What?" she asked, eyes bleary. I felt guilty, but there was no going back now.

"I...I have something important to tell you. Do you mind if I come into your room for a bit?"

"Mm...go ahead..."

Her permission came shockingly easy. She tottered through the doorway. I hurried after her before the door automatically locked itself.

As the corner room, 201 had large windows on the east and south sides, but there was no skyline to look at now. The room was maybe 175 square feet and had standard furniture: a bed that was spacious enough for one but not two, a sofa set, and a writing desk. The floor was dark brown but checkered in that familiar eight-inch pattern.

Asuna floated weightlessly to the bed and plopped down onto its soft surface. She waited for me to speak, just barely preventing herself from flopping over into a sleeping position.

"So what's this important thing you have to...tell......Important thing?" she repeated, blinking thrice.

Suddenly, her eyes were wide open. She stared around the room, then back at me. For some reason, her left hand reached for a large pillow, and she clutched it in front of her as she stammered, "Uh...wait...import...I...W-wait, I'm, uh, I'm not, ready for..."

It wasn't clear what Asuna was imagining, but fortunately for me, whatever it was had woken her up a bit. I took a step closer.

"Listen, Asuna."

"No, wa...w-wait, just wait."

"No. I can't wait."

"What?"

She was clutching the pillow so hard it was fit to burst. I took another step closer.

"Asuna…in the morning, I want you to practice human combat with me."

"………Hweh?"

"I know you hate PvP. But we're coming to the point where there's no getting around it. Before we start heading out to tackle this floor, we should at least spend half a day practicing…"

"Stop."

Her hand darted out at the speed of lightning, cutting me off. She took several deep breaths. Eventually, she got to her feet, still holding the pillow.

"……I knew that I couldn't keep running away from it. So I agree with your point about the training. I'm ready for it."

"Oh…c-cool."

"But let me just say one thing first."

The fencer grinned at me kindly, switched the pillow over to her right hand, then cocked it back.

"That was…*extremely* misleading!!!!" she screamed, hurling it at me overhand with a bit of rotation, like a major league pitcher. The pillow hurtled audibly toward me hard enough to flash up the purple barrier effect when it landed, no matter how soft it was.

A cold drink of water helped calm Asuna down, after which I briefly explained what had happened in the castle ruins of Karluin. While she was furious at necro-poncho—and somewhat concerned for me as well—she largely accepted the situation calmly and rationally and agreed to resume dueling practice.

By the end of this, it was already 3:40, so we delayed the next day's meeting until nine thirty, and I left Room 201.

Suddenly, the sandman's bags weighed heavily on my eyelids, now that I was no longer holding him at bay with sheer willpower. But there was another job I had to do before I opened the door to my own room.

Unlike Room 201, the fifteen puzzle to open Room 202 had a

pair of twos, and the highest number was thirteen. While I did make a few mistakes because of it, I managed to finish the puzzle in under thirty seconds. I opened the door into my own room, removed my gear as I shuffled forward, and plunged into the bed face-first.

I had time for just a few thoughts in the three seconds before I fell asleep.

*You know, I forgot to actually tell Asuna that the entire theme of this floor is puzzles.*

*And what did she mean by "misleading"?*

# 2

DESPITE THE FACT THAT I FORGOT TO SET A WAKE-UP alarm, my eyes opened just three minutes before we were scheduled to meet.

In the real world, I'd never make it in time with that little to spare, but in here, there was no need to wash your face, brush your hair, or pick out what to wear. I just rolled out of bed, equipped the coat over my shirt, and left the room.

The sound of the door opening and slamming was louder than I expected, and for a moment, I wondered if I was still a bit dazed with sleep. But no, my fellow guest in the room next door had emerged at the exact same time.

Asuna and I shared a look for about two seconds. It seemed like she'd just woken up, too, and her brain wasn't running at full capacity yet. In the silence, I heard the number plates of both doors click and rattle as they shuffled their puzzles.

"Good—" I started to say, but Asuna swept her cape aside and raced past me toward the stairs.

*Why did she run away?!*

But the answer occurred to me immediately. She was going to get to the restaurant a second ahead of me, so she could smugly accuse *me* of being the one who slept in.

"N-no fair!" I shouted, starting to run, but I couldn't catch up to Asuna at full speed, given her (likely) higher agility stat. Her long hair shone in the morning sun as it vanished around the end of the hallway.

I was going to lose the race.

Resigned to bad behavior, I launched myself off the floor and took one, two, three steps along the nearest wall, dragging the edges of my soles along the flat stone. This was a non-system skill I called Wall-Running. Three steps was the best I could do without an equipment bonus, but with an Agility dump stat, people like Argo the Rat could probably go much longer.

Still, it was enough to get me to the corner of the hallway, so on my third step, I pushed hard and leaped to the far wall around the corner, then jumped off that to the handrail on the stairs. I landed right behind Asuna, who'd slowed down at the hallway turn that sat at the stairs' landing. With one more huge jump, I slipped past her and rushed into the first-floor lobby.

"Hey, no fair!" she shouted behind me, but athletic competition was inherently unfair. The entrance to the restaurant was past the reception desk. I lowered my center of gravity in preparation for the last fifty feet of the race—

"*Hi-yah!*" went an unsettling cry over my shoulder, and I felt myself being pulled backward. My soles lost their grip and slid along the polished floor. Asuna had grabbed the hem of my coat.

"Hey…foul! Foul!" I wailed as I fell onto my butt, but there was no referee's whistle.

Right beside my face, I heard her say "Later!" as white leather boots raced past me.

Yes—there were no rules or referees in this battle. Only our good consciences limited what we would do. And I was the kind of person who was furthest from the concept of a good conscience: I was a teenage boy and a former beta tester.

I reached out without a word and grabbed Asuna's left ankle.

"Heywha?!" the fencer exclaimed, a strange abbreviation of *Hey, what are you doing?* and she lost her balance. A second after we both rolled over onto the floor, the NPC lady behind the counter called out, "Please, no disruptions inside the building." If it wasn't my imagination, her voice seemed colder than usual.

We sat at the farthest table in the back of the restaurant and ordered the breakfast platters and coffee.

Asuna sighed. "Haaah…The last thing I need in the morning is to get all tired out…"

"W-well, you were the one who started running first."

"I was just picking up my pace, that's all."

I knew she was lying, but the food arrived before I could call her out on it. The breakfast platter varied depending on the town and establishment; this one had two buttered rolls, green salad, cheese, ham, and eggs, which was a fairly orthodox combination.

Asuna neatly sliced the square of cheese into two triangles and noted, "You don't have to solve a puzzle to get your food."

"Oh, would you prefer it that way? For lunch, I know a place that sells a meal served in a puzzle box…"

"No, thank you," she said, picking up the hard cheese with her fingers and taking a nibble. We ate in silence after that, and it wasn't until the both of us were half-done with our plates that Asuna spoke again.

"…So why are there so many puzzles all over Stachion?"

"Oh. It's because the theme of this floor is puzzles," I said, finally revealing the detail I'd forgotten to tell her last night. The fencer blinked in surprise.

"You mean…it's not just the main town, but it's the entire floor that's like this?"

"Yep. Most of the dungeons are full of puzzles and tricks. It was a floor that really divided the player base during the beta, I can tell you that."

"Uh…huh…"

There was something odd in Asuna's look, but with my low Communication skill, I couldn't make out what it was.

"...What does that expression mean?" I asked her, sticking ham inside of the slit in my mini-loaf of hard bread. Asuna shrugged.

"Well, it's not that I hate puzzles themselves...I like the sudoku number games from the square—and jigsaw puzzles and disentanglement puzzles and the like. But...when I think about the fifth-floor boss, I get worried..."

"Oh. Good point..."

At last, I understood why she looked upset. The floor boss we'd just defeated yesterday—Fuscus the Vacant Colossus—started off like your archetypal RPG golem monster but turned out to be horribly different—a creature fused with the very chamber itself. It then deployed a number of complex gimmicks and tricks that were a huge headache for the raid party.

"So does that mean if the floor's theme is puzzles that the boss is the same way?" Asuna asked.

"Kind of," I admitted. "The boss in the beta was kind of like a Rubik's Cube with arms and legs. The row you attacked would rotate, and once you got all the sides aligned, its armor would break off. But because everyone just went ham on it, the colors would get more and more out of alignment..."

"..."

Asuna sighed deeply, her fork paused in midair with a cucumber-like vegetable on it. "That's exactly the kind of thing that Lind from the DKB and Kibaou from the ALS are going to argue over—who gets to call the shots in battle. Maybe it's better that we tackle this boss with the same group as the last one?"

It was bold, but I had to shake the idea off. "No, no way. We had no other choice in the matter to prevent the ALS from rushing ahead...but the entire point of boss fights is to use a full raid party and go in at maximum strength. And you never know if it might've been changed since the beta."

"Probably to make it *more* annoying, if anything."

This time I had to agree. I didn't want to imagine a setup more annoying than the Rubik's Cube, but if any pattern had held true so far, it was that nothing had been made easier since the beta.

On top of that, I had another problem to deal with regarding the boss battle beyond just the potential puzzle tricks.

Asuna sensed something in my expression. She chewed on a slice of cucumber and waved her fork like a little flag. "Speaking of which…what are you going to do with that thing you're holding?"

"Dunno," I said. She made a face that said she figured that was the answer.

The "thing" I was holding was the Flag of Valor, an ultrarare item that the fifth-floor boss dropped—otherwise known as the guild flag.

If you registered the flag under your guild name and stood it upright on the floor, any guild member within a radius of fifty feet would enjoy four different kinds of status buffing. The reason Kibaou's ALS had attempted to sneak into a fight against the boss first was because they were afraid the DKB would get the guild flag and the incredible bonus it conferred.

But the impromptu raid party that Asuna and I had scraped together beat the fifth-floor boss first, and the flag in question came into my possession. Lind probably didn't know about the very existence of the flag yet, so I was going to set up a meeting with the chief DKB members later that day to explain everything. Understanding the man's pride, there was no telling how he would react.

When Kibaou barged into the boss chamber right after we defeated Fuscus, I gave him the conditions that would need to be fulfilled before I handed over the guild flag.

One: I would hold on to the flag until another one of them showed up, at which point I'd give it up so that the ALS and DKB would each have one.

Or two: If the ALS and DKB merged, I would give them the flag immediately.

Either one of these would be satisfactory to me, but I knew that neither was a realistic outcome. It was such a game-changing item that players called it "broken," so there wouldn't be multiple copies of that kind of thing dropping left and right—in the beta, only the one on the fifth floor ever showed up. And the DKB and ALS, who held opposing ideologies, merging into one? Even more unlikely.

"...If we give the flag to either guild, it'll destroy the balance we've got now. It'll permanently destroy any chance at peace between the two sides, and in the worst-case scenario, it could wipe out half the power of the frontier-advancing group," I mumbled, staring at the parsley-like green left on my plate. I sensed Asuna nodding along. Then I plucked up the leafy thing and twirled it in my fingers. "But it's also so powerful that letting it rot away in my inventory would be a waste...At the present moment, we have hardly any means of adding combat buffs, and this will provide four different kinds, just from sticking a flag into the ground..."

"What specific buffs, exactly?"

"Increased attack power, increased defensive power, shortened cooldowns, and increased resistance to all debuffs."

"Wow..."

He₁ voice was hushed with awe. Asuna was still new to the general concepts of RPGs, but even she could recognize what tremendous benefits this combination of effects represented.

"Of course, in sheer numerical terms, the individual values are pretty small, but it can also affect any number of players—and for an unlimited amount of time...And the craziest part of all is that the guild flag itself is categorized as a polearm weapon with a number of possible upgrade attempts..."

"Oh...h-how many?"

"Ten."

Again, an incredulous look crossed Asuna's face. "And...I'm guessing...that's not to increase its power as a weapon, but..."

"It should also affect the buffing percentages. I'm almost afraid to imagine what it would be like if you successfully upgraded it all ten times."

"Hrmmm," the fencer grunted uncharacteristically. She pointed her fork and knife at me. "Then what about this idea?"

"What's that?"

"Why don't you start a new guild, register the flag, and absorb both the DKB and ALS?"

A sound that if transcribed would be spelled something like *blrmpph* shot from my mouth. Thankfully, I avoided spraying half-chewed parsley mist into Asuna's face, but something seemed very buggy in the game's taste emulator—my mouth felt weirdly textured. I took a swig of coffee to reset, inhaled and exhaled several times, then expressed myself more rationally this time.

"Absolutely not. Zero percent chance. Zero-point-zero-zero-zero-zero!"

"……"

The look on her face said *What are you, a child?* She took a delicate sip of her coffee. "It was only a suggestion. I know it's not to your liking, and I have no desire at all to be the subleader of any guild. The most practical version of the idea would be to ask Agil…but even that seems unlikely to work…"

She lapsed into silence, thinking hard. I considered asking if she would actually agree to be my vice-captain in a hypothetical guild, but I wasn't sure it was a good idea to bring up. I decided to keep it locked away in my mental inventory for now.

"…Well, Agil's already leading a guild of his own…but if we had him expand the Bro Squad into a larger organization, I feel like he'd force them all to use two-handed weapons…"

"Ah-ha-ha-ha, no way." Asuna laughed, only to suddenly stop. She must've imagined herself as a member of the Bro Squad, wielding a huge war hammer. She shook her head. "A-anyway, we ought to think of a way to effectively use that guild flag. Let's hope that Lind has some constructive ideas in mind…"

"Yeah, no kidding…"

At that, the clock hit ten. Our meeting with the DKB was at twelve thirty and would be held somewhere in Stachion. So factoring in travel time, that left us with about two hours to kill. I tossed the last scrap of bread into my mouth, mumbled a thanks for the meal, and gave my partner a suggestion.

"Um, to round out the morning, why don't we go all over Sta-chion, accept all the quests we can, and clear out one or two of the easy ones? Or we can practice dueling, like we talked about yesterday. Which do you prefer?"

"Hmm," Asuna murmured, but her answer came very quickly. "Practice. I don't want to put it off and then regret it later."

"Oh…c-cool," I said, taken aback by her choice. "In that case, let's find somewhere we can be alone. If people overhear or spy on our practice, it'll only have the opposite effect."

"Sounds good…but do you have a place in mind?"

"I might." I grinned, leaping to my feet.

Unlike last night, the teleport square was bustling with players. More than a few had parchment and quill in hand, staring at the numbered tiles. It wasn't yet clear if these were going to be the new generation of sudokers, but I wished them a silent good luck and hopped through the glowing blue gate at the center of the square.

Our destination was Zumfut, the main town of the third floor. But the town itself was not what I wanted. I led us right past the three giant baobab trees out into the map and off the trail. Once I was certain there were no players following us, I took us at a sprint southwest, into the deep forest.

Monsters targeted us now and then, but at this point, Asuna and I were strong enough that an ambush of small treants or giant spiders in the Forest of Wavering Mists needed no more than two sword skills to clean up. We ignored them and contin-ued running, leaving them all in the dust.

Eventually, a valley came into view, the mist trailing through it in ropes even thicker than usual. I left my map open and contin-ued running right through the valley for another minute.

Suddenly, the mist vanished like it had never been there, and tall black banners appeared before my eyes. They featured a scimitar and a horn, and beyond them was a hollow in the valley, inside of which were nearly twenty dark purple tents of various sizes. But this was no ordinary village—it was the campground of the dark elf warriors, a place that only players aligned with the dark elf faction of the multi-floor "Elf War" campaign quest could visit. On top of that, it was an instanced map generated for each separate party, meaning the game system itself prevented any other player from even seeing it, much less getting inside.

Asuna bowed to the expressionless guards as she passed them, then murmured to me, "It's been over ten days since we were last here. It's nice to be back…but why now? Are you saying there's nowhere private we could find in Stachion or Karluin?"

"There are…but there was one other thing I wanted to clean up."

"What's that…? Isn't the next destination for the 'Elf War' quest on the sixth floor?"

I nodded. The general story of the campaign, which had started on this floor, was that the dark elves and forest elves were fighting for six secret keys that opened the gate to a place called the Sanctuary that existed somewhere in Aincrad. But behind this conflict lurked the Fallen Elves, who were secretly after the keys as well.

We'd gained the Jade Key on the third floor, the Lapis Key on the fourth, and the Amber Key on the fifth. The elite dark elf knight Kizmel used a spirit tree, a special means of travel just for the elves, to transport the keys to a fortress in the northwest region of the sixth floor, where they were stored now. Once we reached that fort, the sixth-floor portion of the campaign would launch—but I had stuff to take care of before we did that.

"This errand has nothing to do with any quests. I just wanna power this guy up," I said, reaching behind me to brush the hilt of my sword. Asuna murmured in understanding.

In the center of the long hollow in the valley was the massive dining tent, in front of which was a tiny commerce area. Along the path was an item shop, a tailor, a leatherworker, and a blacksmith. It looked the same as it did the last time we visited, except that the normally passive and brusque elves actually called out to us this time, greeting us and asking how we were. I was so taken aback by this that all I could do was nod back, but Asuna flashed them a smile and said, "Good day!"

I guessed that some kind of affinity value with the dark elves was rising as we proceeded further in the campaign quest, and that it meant our fame and wanted value among the forest elves was rising along with it. We hadn't interacted with them on the fifth floor, so I just had to pray that the pattern would hold for the sixth as well.

I stopped us at the fourth shop in the row. Out in front was a stern-looking man wearing a heavy apron and long gloves, his hair tied in a ponytail, beating a piece of red-hot metal on top of an anvil with rhythmic strikes. After the change in the other elves, I assumed he would be more friendly as well, so I waited for a pause in the work before calling out, "H...hiya!"

The man glared at us, snorted, then went back to work.

"...Well, he hasn't changed a bit," whispered Asuna, holding back her giggles, but I wouldn't be broken yet.

I took the entire sheath off my back and said, "Um, I'd like to strengthen this sword."

He snorted again. The only indication this wasn't a refusal of my request was that a special NPC blacksmith window had appeared before me.

*I swear, I'm gonna get this guy to like me someday,* I thought as I entered my work request into the window.

My Anneal Blade +8 had been my trusty sidekick since shortly after the start of this game of death, but it broke in half in the fight against the forest elf commander during the battle at Yofel Castle on the fourth floor. Now I was using the Sword of Eventide, a one-handed longsword that had been a reward for winning that fight. On top of its excellent base stats, it had a magic effect that added +7 agility. With it equipped, my ability to Wall-Run stretched from three steps at best all the way to nearly ten.

However, powerful weapons were also difficult to upgrade as a general rule. So I'd been using it without attempting to increase its power all through the fifth floor. Now that we were going to tackle the sixth, I wanted to at least get it up to +3. And as far as I knew, the best NPC blacksmith I could call upon was this fellow. With skill like his, a little unfriendliness wasn't going to be a problem...I hoped.

I set the materials that matched my weapon type on the menu screen and paused to think when I reached the additive materials section.

The weapon-upgrading system in *SAO* allowed you to choose between five different parameters: Sharpness, Heaviness, Quickness, Accuracy, and Durability. Sharpness (or Toughness for blunt weapons) simply increased its damage, and Heaviness increased the chances of breaking an opponent's weapon or armor. Quickness improved the speed of regular attacks and sword skills, while Accuracy improved the critical rate, and Durability increased the weapon's own ability to withstand damage. Any of them would be an improvement, but the smart move was to choose values that matched your combat style. I often chose Sharpness and Durability for my upgrades, because they didn't interface with system assistance the way the others did.

I decided I would go for Sharpness twice and Durability once, so I selected the maximum number of additional materials that corresponded to Sharpness, then hit the OK button. When dealing with a player blacksmith, you had to manually choose the needed materials and extras from your own inventory, but with an NPC, it was all automatic. A little bag filled with the materials appeared over the window. I held it out with one hand and grasped my sword with the other, then I asked the blacksmith to go ahead.

But the elf ignored the bag of materials in my hand and took just the sword. He pulled it from the sheath and let the blade catch the morning sunlight. A little furrow appeared between his brows.

"...Is this the work of a Lyusulan master?" he asked abruptly. At first, I panicked, wondering if this was the start of some in-game event, but I had to be honest at this point. The kingdom of Lyusula was the dark elf nation that existed on the land before Aincrad was created, and they still called themselves the people of Lyusula.

"Y-yes...I received it from the master of Yofel Castle on the fourth floor."

"Ahh, a piece from Leyshren's family, then."

I leaned over to Asuna, feeling like I'd probably heard that name before, and whispered, "Uh...who was that again?"

"Come on, pay attention and remember things. That was the name of Viscount Yofilis."

"Oh, right," I said, but then I frowned, uncertain. The blacksmith had just referred to that dark elf noble by his first name in a rather casual manner, but I couldn't tell if that was a notable thing or if it was simply the customary way of their culture.

He didn't seem to pay any attention to our whispers, though. He continued examining the beautiful sword. "You ordered an improvement to Sharpness, correct?"

"Yes, to start with."

"Don't bother."

"......Huh?"

Now I was truly stunned. I could feel my eyes and mouth bulging wide. Old Man Romolo, the shipwright who built our gondola on the fourth floor, had been somewhat of a crank by NPC standards, but even he didn't outright refuse a request for his services. Yet the elf blacksmith was going to turn down the order that I'd entered through the system menu itself. He'd never uttered a word of complaint when I had him augment the Sharpness of the Anneal Blade...

"Um...wh-why not?" I asked.

The blacksmith snorted with obvious annoyance, but at least this time he did explain himself. "This sword is already sharp enough. Sharpening it further will not improve it."

"I...see..."

I guessed that meant that compared to the Anneal Blade, giving it +1 Sharpness would only provide a small extra boost of attack power.

It was true that weapon upgrading ought to be appropriate

for the type of weapon. Boosting the Quickness of a massive two-handed war hammer once or twice would barely register any change in speed—and increasing the Heaviness of a quick rapier or dagger would only wipe out its special nature without improving its ability to destroy other weapons and armor.

But I'd never considered that there might be individual tendencies among different weapons in the same one-handed sword category when it came to upgrading. Taken aback, I asked him, "Then what kind of improvement would you recommend?"

"Choose whichever quality you like, aside from Sharpness…is what I might ordinarily say, but if Leyshren owed you enough to give you this, I suppose you deserve keener advice," he said icily. The blacksmith gazed closely at the Sword of Eventide again. "Accuracy would be good for this sword."

"Awww…" I blurted out like a petulant child.

Upgrading Accuracy increased a weapon's critical rate: This much was undeniable fact. The problem was that the debate about just *what* a critical hit was in *SAO* hadn't been settled yet.

Many monsters had defined weak points, which, if hit cleanly, suffered huge damage. Nearly all players understood this to be a critical hit.

But aside from that, when hitting non-weak spots, there was a very rare chance that the striking effect would be just a bit flashier than usual—and deliver just a bit more damage. It was easier to do this with sword skills than normal attacks, but it was also not the same thing as the "power boost" technique you could take advantage of by throwing your arms and legs further into the movements the system helped you make automatically during a sword skill. This was something where the exact same sword skill in the exact same spot on the enemy might or might not cause the effect—it was completely up to chance.

If you listened to the critical hit fundamentalists who'd been studying crits since the beta (we called them critters), hitting an enemy's weak point was a skill, and major damage scored through player skill was not a critical. They were searching for that random extra damage roll, the true critical hit from RPGs of yore—the thing that couldn't be affected by clever technique.

Beyond this point was a bottomless swamp of data, idealism, and cultish fanaticism from which escape was nearly impossible. The critters would tell you that a true critical was determined by how truly serious the NerveGear detected the player was; that it was easier to score the more wood your weapon contained; that the fewer HP you had left, the higher the rate; that a full moon increased your chances; and on and on...There wasn't enough time or life to rigorously test any or all of these theories.

And in all honesty, I had no desire to get anywhere near that swamp, but the problem was that I knew there *were* true criticals that were different from weak-point criticals. The pleasure of seeing the 20-percent exaggerated effect and major damage was addicting once you got used to it. I wasn't a critter by a long shot, but on the other hand, I'd been keeping my modification slot open for the five days since I reached 150 proficiency in one-handed swords because I couldn't choose whether I wanted Shortened Skill Delay or Critical Rate Increase, which I had to assume affected the chances of a true crit.

You'd think that if it was this tempting, I should just go for the critical rate boost, but the problem was that upgrading weapon Accuracy affected only weak-point criticals, not true criticals.

When a weapon's Accuracy had been boosted, the system automatically adjusted to improve your aim when trying to hit a monster's weak spot. Some players, like Asuna, could master this system and use it like second nature. But I didn't hang with any kind of system assistance that took control away from me. During the beta test, I tried out an Anneal Blade with Accuracy increased to +8, and the sensation of the sword curving straight for the monster's weak spot made me feel like I was wielding a living weapon with a mind of its own.

So...how was I supposed to explain to the dark elf this very particular quirk of mine, based on preference rather than rational gain? If I insisted on Sharpness, that might solve the matter, but it seemed like there was a 1—no, a 10-percent chance that this particular NPC would say "*Then I won't do it.*" Instead, I just glanced back and forth between the sword and his face.

Finally, Asuna broke the stalemate with a perfect, simple solution.

"Why isn't Sharpness the best choice?" she asked.

The blacksmith nodded. "Of all of Lyusula's great blades, this one is especially sharp—and thus fragile. To preserve and protect the blade, it is best to dispatch the enemy with as few strikes as possible. That means Accuracy would be best, followed by Durability."

"Ah, I see…So the Accuracy is to make fighting more efficient," Asuna said, echoing my own reaction.

The sword's Durability wasn't bad at all according to its specs, but ever since I'd started using it, I noticed that it seemed to deplete on the quick side in battle. The Sword of Eventide was better at slicing away at uncovered or undefended spots than at smashing through layers of armor, presumably. If one focused on hitting weak points from the very start, then the effect of the system assistance kicking in might not be that disorienting, after all.

It hadn't eliminated all of my misgivings, but if this was a sword forged by a dark elf, it was probably best to accept a dark elf blacksmith's advice about it. "Okay…I understand. Then let's upgrade its Accuracy, please," I said.

"Very well," the blacksmith replied, and the window popped up once more. I reset the items and values, hit the ok button again, and grabbed the bag of materials that appeared.

The blacksmith took the items and tossed them into the furnace that seemed to be made of wood. The materials melted instantly, and the orange flames began to glow blue. He stuck the Sword of Eventide in, and it promptly took on a blue glow of its own.

Then he transferred the sword to the anvil—I couldn't tell why he chose the specific timing of it—and began to smack it with his hammer. With just ten strikes, quick enough that I didn't have time to get nervous, the sword promptly flashed brighter.

"It is done," he said, thrusting the sword toward me.

"Um," I said without taking it, "I'd like another round of Accuracy, actually, followed by Durability."

Even maximizing the amount of materials you could put into the process, upgrading couldn't get higher than a 95-percent chance of success, but the blacksmith easily cranked out three perfect attempts. It was my nature to want to keep the streak going, but that was sadly the end of my stock of mats. I still had three moo-moo planks (the cow-branded metal pieces) that could boost your chances to maximum in one go, but I was saving them for when it was really necessary.

Instead, Asuna decided to get up to +7 on her Chivalric Rapier—the scary part was that she still had eight attempts left—and then we thanked the blacksmith, who gave us a disinterested snort and returned to his business. I was curious about why he called Viscount Yofilis by the name Leyshren, but we didn't have time, so that would have to wait for another day.

We also stopped at the leatherworker and the seamstress for some upgrades to our armor—both of these were women and at least five times friendlier than the smith. When this was done, Asuna and I moved to the outdoor training grounds at the western end of the encampment. It was now 10:40, so even accounting for travel, we had a full hour to practice.

There was no way I could teach her every little trick and lesson I'd picked up over my time with the game, and that was likely to backfire with Asuna anyway. Teaching her more about the essentials, about the mind-set that one needed, was far more likely to help her make use of her own creativity and proactive capabilities.

The problem was that giving a lecture on mental outlook was much harder than talking about technique. And it was all the more difficult when the teacher was just a dumb kid like me with no experience teaching.

I came to a stop at the entrance to the empty training grounds, glanced at Asuna, who was standing at a thirty-degree angle from me, and came up completely short on how to start even the first sentence. All I could think about was the way Asuna had said *I don't want to do this* when we tried practicing dueling on the fourth floor.

"Soooo……ummmm……"

I hemmed and hawed, trying to find an entry point to the topic.

Suddenly, Asuna giggled and said, "Listen, Kirito."

"Y…yes?"

"I went into the bath with Argo when we were in the town of Shiyaya on the fifth floor."

"Y…yes?"

It sounded familiar to me, I just couldn't wrap my head around why she was bringing it up now. I looked at her suspiciously. "R-right, I seem to recall that. You and Argo were having a little girl-on-girl chat in the…"

"We were doing no such thing!" she said, pouting briefly. Then she grinned. "No, Argo and I had a duel there."

"……Wha—? In the…bath?"

"In the bath."

"……With…no gear?"

"With swimsui…Wait, that's not the point!"

She jabbed me in the gut with her first two fingers pressed together. Belatedly, I recalled that we weren't in a town safe zone—but to my relief, she didn't do anything worse than that.

"…But when I say duel, all we did was smack each other with the bundles of fragrant herbs they put in the bathtub. Argo asked me…if I was afraid of dueling."

"…A-and what did you say…?"

"I was honest. I told her I was scared, but thinking on it, Argo uses all of her points for agility, so she's got even less HP than me. Yet, in the duel, she fought hard with just a bundle of plants and didn't seem nervous at all. She heads into the latest dungeon without an ounce of hesitation…So in return, I asked her, 'Aren't you afraid?'"

"……A-a-and she said…?"

"'Fraid I can't tell ya that for free,'" Asuna said, a remarkable imitation of Argo the Rat's speaking style, and headed for the other end of the grounds.

I called out after her. "Um, c-could you explain what that story is supposed to mean?"

The fencer turned back, her long hair swishing, and gave me a devilish grin. "What do *you* suppose it means?"

*How the hell should I know?!* I shouted inwardly. Chances were, Asuna was trying to say that she was all right now. So I just had to teach her as much as I could in the short time we had. Once she got over her fear of fighting another human player, there was nothing left to hold back Asuna's potential and the sharp point of her +7 Chivalric Rapier.

I glanced up at the forest surrounding the camp and whispered a warning to the man in the black poncho and his friends, wherever in Aincrad they were now.

"Next time I'm gonna get you."

"Huh? Did you say something?" Asuna shouted.

"Nothing!" I shouted back, hurrying over the short grass toward my partner.

# 3

WHEN WE RETURNED TO STACHION, THE TELEPORT square was jammed with players. The majority looked like tourists from the first floor, but there were also a surprising number of "catchers-up" loaded with fairly decent gear.

This second group had gotten off to a start a month or two later than the present-day advancement group and weren't a high enough level to hang in the frontier zones, but shopping in town was perfectly safe. And since it was RPG custom that the further a town was in the game, the better its equipment, every new destination was a chance to buy into a better round of gear—if you could afford it.

In that sense, Kibaou's Aincrad Liberation Squad and their stated aims of sharing money, items, and information as widely as possible weren't wrong. If the frontline groups used their earnings to help outfit the people catching up, they'd be able to gain XP more safely—and reach the frontier much quicker.

But the actual method of distribution was rather tricky. It wasn't as if the advancement group was drowning in money, so you'd only want to distribute money to those players who were truly serious about reaching the front line. But in order to identify them from the rest, you'd need to do some time-consuming background checks and skill tests. Even the large ALS didn't have the man power to bother with something that involved, and if they did, acting like heavy-handed police or military might only inspire mistrust instead.

When I beat everyone to the punch by defeating the fifth-floor boss and looting the guild flag first, Kibaou quietly thanked me. He must've understood that we were forced to do this to prevent the coalition of frontline groups from fracturing. He might have a foul mouth, but he wasn't a bad person. It was why he was so dedicated to the noble cause of redistributing resources to give everyone a fair shot.

On the other hand, Lind of the Dragon Knights Brigade was the polar opposite—a man who proposed concentrating resources instead. He wanted to create a band of heroes who would accumulate all the money and gear and experience, shining bright at the forefront of the game. The idea was that this would inspire the lower players to work even harder in the hopes of joining his team—a choice of ideals that seemed at odds with reality.

But one thing was certain: If the unique guild flag item was going to work better in either the ALS or DKB, it would clearly be the latter. And Asuna and I needed to explain the flag's crazy effects to Lind's guild, as well as the requirements for us to actually give it up.

"…Just five more minutes now…Have they settled on a place?" Asuna asked after she emerged from the teleporter. I checked my instant messages.

"It says we're meeting at an inn called the Pegasus Hoof. It's that one over there," I said, using my memory from the beta to point at a white building on the north side of the square. It was much bigger than the Fifteen Numbers, where we were staying.

Stachion was arranged like a gentle series of steps, with the northern side being higher and the southern sinking lower. I used the word *steps* rather than *hill* because the ground was made up of those eight-inch cube tiles, so there was no natural slope to be found. It wasn't as simple as just uniform steps lined up across the entire town, but if you traveled north and south enough, you would undoubtedly find yourself going up and down stairs.

As we walked toward the inn, Asuna looked up at the north side and asked, "So...who lives in the biggest building up at the north end?"

"That's the lord's mansion. He's, uh, a guy named Cylon, with a beard. He gives you a bunch of quests, so we'll be there a few times. It gets real tiring climbing all those stairs, though...There's just something mentally draining about stairs, as opposed to an ordinary hill."

Asuna didn't comment on any of that. She frowned and murmured, "Cylon...Where have I heard that name before...?"

"Wasn't that the bad guy from *The Lord of the Rings*?"

"That was Sauron, dummy...Well, whatever. How many minutes to go?"

"Um...one minute, twenty-two seconds."

"They're going to be so conceited if we're late. Let's run!"

The fencer tore off down the tiles for our destination, and I had to rush to keep up. We passed through the large door of the Pegasus Hoof at seven seconds before twelve thirty, but the blue-haired man seated on the sofa in the lobby promptly and loudly said, "You're late. It's common practice to arrive for any meeting five minutes before the agreed-upon time."

If we were going to get sniped at one way or the other, I wished we'd come five minutes *late*. Instead, I had no choice but to wave at Lind, leader of the Dragon Knights Brigade guild, and his officers Shivata and Hafner. "Yo. You guys eat already?"

As young as they might have looked, they were at least in their late teens, so as a middle schooler, I ought to have asked, *"Did you gentlemen already enjoy your lunchtime?"* But this was Aincrad, the land of outlaws. On top of that, people seemed to think I was two, three, maybe even four or five years older than I really was, so the only thing all that extra verbiage would do was clog up my online connection with voice data.

Lind didn't seem bothered by my attitude. It was more the content of the message he took offense to, a furrow running through his brow.

"We have been waiting here for fifteen minutes already. Where would we find that kind of time?"

It seemed to me like that was plenty of time, but I decided to keep it friendly and suggested, "Then why don't we talk over a meal? You're just going to head right back out for more adventuring in the afternoon, aren't you?"

This was a profound bit of strategizing by my standards, hoping that Lind's attitude might soften over some good food, but the blue-haired guild master shook his head. "No, I don't want any chance that we'll be overheard...We're going to talk in a room that my guild has reserved for the purpose."

"...Got it," I said after a pause. If Lind was renting the room, no one else might be able to unlock the door, but it would still open from the inside, and we were within the town, so they couldn't do anything to hold us there by force. I didn't think the leader of a powerful guild would stoop to such a thing, but the guild flag had all the magical allure of the One Ring, so I had to be careful.

Lind rose from his seat and took Shivata and Hafner—whom I secretly nicknamed the track athlete and soccer player, respectively—toward a staircase at the back of the lobby. If anything, Lind seemed like a member of the calligraphy club, although that might've just been because the back of his ponytail looked like the tip of a brush to me.

As I followed the trio, I couldn't keep my mind from wandering over some truly pointless subjects. *Maybe, if I really need to write something on parchment, and I have ink but no quill pen, I could dip that tail into the ink and...*

They led us to the Pegasus Hoof's third-floor suite. It seemed like a sure sign that they were a big, wealthy guild...except one thing stuck out to me.

"Hey, guys, did you go into this room ahead of time?" I asked, right before we reached the door.

Lind turned around and answered peevishly, "No, we just rented the room at the desk."

"I see...so you haven't tried this puzzle yet." I pointed at a very complicated, messy metal object placed in an alcove next to the door.

"What's that?" Hafner wondered, raising a thick eyebrow. But Asuna seemed to have recognized what the object was.

"Where did the DKB stay last night?" she asked them.

"Well, we were having fun as a group at the year-end party... and we ended up passing out at the room in Karluin where we were celebrating. We didn't come up to the sixth floor until this morning."

"I see."

Asuna shot me a glance. Apparently, explaining the situation was my job, so I cleared my throat.

"Well, I'm sure you've noticed that this town—in fact, this entire floor—is covered in puzzles...and so are the inns. Pretty much every inn requires you to solve some kind of puzzle before you can open your room door. The type varies depending on the establishment, and the Pegasus Hoof specializes in cast metal puzzles...which are like big, heavy disentanglement puzzles. The cheapest rooms are fairly simple horseshoe puzzles, but the more expensive the inn, the trickier they get..."

"............"

The track, soccer, and calligraphy club members stared at the metal object in the wall niche. After they traded a series of looks that suggested *No, you go first*, Shivata gave up and reached for it.

The puzzle was three tightly interlocked U-shaped parts with little protrusions like deer antlers on them. Two of the parts were chained to the wall, and the third had the door key stuck to it. It would not come loose unless it slid off at just the right position and angle. It must've taken quite a lot of precision and data to re-create such a complex puzzle with 3-D models.

Shivata rattled the puzzle for about thirty seconds before he threw up his hands and backed away. Hafner didn't even last for twenty. Lind was third, positively glowing with an aura that said *For the glory of the guild!*

Observing from a distance of six feet, Asuna whispered to me,

"I guess the name Pegasus Hoof was a hint as to these horseshoe puzzles."

"The fifteen puzzles at our inn were a lot better, huh?"

"Once you figure out the trick, maybe…"

Lind's valiant attempt at the puzzle continued while we chatted, but he, too, came to a stop after about a minute of trying.

"…It is not coming off. Something must be stuck."

"Now, now, Lin, it wouldn't be a true puzzle if there's no solution."

"Then *you* do it, Haf."

"Listen, I'm not good at these things…"

A part of me wanted to keep observing this very rare glimpse at the DKB members acting casually, but the conversation we were supposed to have would be tricky enough as it was, so this was my cue to step in and help.

"Pardon me," I said, barging in with a little hand chop and taking the tangled metal puzzle. It was four months ago that I'd been tackling this town's puzzles in the beta, but the muscle memory for these cast-metal puzzles was still there…I hoped.

At the time, if you fell asleep in an inn bed, the NerveGear automatically logged you out of the dive, so that when you woke up, you were in your real-world room again. The sleep log-out was a popular trick among beta testers because it allowed you to avoid the usual intoxication of emerging from a full dive, but I didn't get to try it more than a few times before the test was over.

In the meantime, I kept my hands moving, slowly getting past one protrusion after another, until the part with the key on it came loose.

"Here." I handed it over to Lind, who looked conflicted about this development. He stuck it into the lock and turned it left. The lock clicked heavily.

"So…what do I do with this n—" he started to ask, but the key rose out of his hand on its own and floated back into the wall niche. It tangled itself back up with the two chained pieces until the puzzle was back to its original position.

"......The heck was that?" asked Shivata.

"It's kind of like magic, kind of like a curse. The lord here will explain it to you," I told him, clapping Lind on the shoulder. "C'mon, let's get this conversation going. I'm sure you're busy, too."

The Pegasus Hoof suite was, indeed, quite deluxe—in addition to a large living room, it had two separate bedrooms, a small kitchen, and a bathroom. Asuna's fixation kicked in briefly as she glanced toward the bathroom door, but given that she had just bathed at the dark elf camp, her bath meter was stable for the moment, and she passed by it without further inspection.

"...Why did you rent such an expensive spot?" I wondered, gazing out the large window at the town of Stachion below.

It wasn't Lind, but it was Hafner who said, "It's an issue of security. If someone just happens to wait outside the door with the Eavesdropping skill, it's more likely that we'll be out of their effective range if the room is extra-large, right?"

"Ah, I see..."

That at least confirmed for me how serious a matter the DKB considered this talk to be. There was a sofa set in the middle of the living area, but Shivata and Hafner decided to move it to the window on the south side out of an abundance of caution, getting it as far from the door as possible. I was going to suggest that they should just post guards outside the door, but then I realized they'd naturally have other members hiding out in the lobby below already.

The furniture set featured a sofa long enough to seat three, and two armchairs. I assumed Asuna and I would take the chairs, but Lind motioned us toward the sofa, so we followed his lead.

Lind and Hafner sat in the armchairs, and Shivata stood to the side. I wasn't sure if they'd decided to have us sit down and then leave one of their own standing as psychological pressure, or if it was just a coincidence.

Abruptly, Hafner said, "Shivata and I explained what happened with the fifth-floor boss to Lind. Including the reason you wanted to get a jump start on the boss, and the reason we decided to participate."

I blinked twice in surprise and said, rather foolishly, "Oh. You did?"

When Shivata and Hafner decided to join our impromptu raid party, they hadn't said anything to Lind, their guild master, about it. I figured we'd either keep that a secret today or use that revelation as the starting point—but it seemed they'd already saved us the trouble.

At that point, we could probably just jump right into it, but Asuna, sitting to my right, shot Shivata a look. I followed her eyesight and saw that the short-haired swordsman was giving us some kind of very awkward signal with his eyes.

I squinted, trying to figure out what message he was trying to send, but Lind noticed my expression and swung around to his right to look at Shivata. Immediately, Asuna said, "Then you must know all about the guild flag already, Lind."

With the mention of the item at the center of everything, Lind turned forward again. "Yes...but only the concept. And I'll be honest—I'm still not sure whether to believe it or not. Before we negotiate, I'd like to see the item first."

The use of the word *negotiate* rather than *discuss* was ominous, but it wasn't enough of a reason to call things off at this stage.

"All right," I said, opening my menu. But before I materialized the item, I decided to set up a safety measure.

First, I went to my equipment mannequin and dragged the icon for the Sword of Eventide +3 from my right-hand slot to my inventory. I'd removed my equipment before we walked into the building, so this action changed nothing about my appearance.

Next, I chose the Flag of Valor from the weapon category of my inventory and dropped it onto my mannequin. It was a two-handed weapon, so the spear icon appeared in both my right- and left-hand slots. Light glowed in my hands before sharpening into the long narrow weapon—er, flag.

When pulling weapons out of item storage, simply choosing to materialize it would pop the item into existence above the window. But if you were equipping it, the weapon appeared in one of two places.

If you had your weapon location selected ahead of time—for a polearm, it was on your back by default—it would appear directly in that spot. But if the setting was still in its initial state, or if you didn't have enough physical space to fit it, the item would appear in your hands instead. Because I had my hands resting atop the window, Lind's group wouldn't be able to tell if I'd just brought the guild flag out as a simple item—or if I was equipping it.

The moment he caught sight of the ten-foot platinum long-spear, Lind's eyes bulged. The butt of the spear reached nearly to the window, while the tip crossed Asuna's knees and jutted out over the end of the sofa. The top quarter of the pole was wrapped in a white cloth, and the string that held it in place was silver. Its stats as a weapon were frankly unimpressive, but the finely carved detail in the handle, the beautiful edging of the flag fabric—the overall informational "weight" of all that detailed data—made it clear this was a special item.

If I'd just taken the flag out in one single step, Lind could grab it and run out of the room. If he escaped for five minutes while Shivata and Hafner prevented me from utilizing the Material-ize All Items command, ownership of the flag would transfer to him. But because I had equipped it first, my period of automatic ownership lasted for a full hour.

I gave the chances of them attempting such a stunt no more than 0.1 percent, but Lind merely tapped the pole to bring up the properties window, read it closely, sighed, and handed it back. He waited for me to put it back into my inventory, then leaned back in his seat and grumbled.

"Yes…I see…Seems like quite the balance-breaking item to have shown up on just the fifth floor…"

"I don't know just how well it works without trying it, though," I admitted.

The guild master shrugged. "The listed properties won't be false. A hundred feet in diameter with four different buffs…Just from that alone, it's almost too powerful to be real. I don't blame Kibaou for trying to slip past the rest of us to get it—even if I find him obnoxious."

He didn't seem as angry as I imagined he might be. Asuna had the same impression.

"Did you already talk with the ALS?" she asked.

"No, we've said nothing. I had a toast with Kibaou at the party last night, but I wasn't aware of the existence of this flag at the time," Lind said, a self-deprecating curl present at the corner of his mouth. He looked to the side, where Hafner was scratching his head guiltily.

That would mean Lind had only heard the explanation in the last few hours. So perhaps the fact that he was so calm and cool about it was a sign that, like Kibaou, as long as the other guild didn't have it, he was fine with the matter. I certainly prayed so.

"Well, now that you've seen it for yourself, I'm going to explain the conditions under which I would hand it over," I continued. "Naturally, they're the same conditions I gave the ALS. Situation one is if another guild flag drops somewhere. If it's going to happen, I'm sure either the ALS or DKB will get it this time, so in this event, I would hand the flag to whichever guild did not get the drop, free of any charge. Situation two is if the ALS and DKB merge guilds. If that happens, I will hand over the flag unconditionally."

When I'd suggested these to the ALS in the fifth-floor boss chamber, they'd yelled at me: *That'll never happen!* and *You gotta be joking!* But Lind might've known about them already, because he barely batted an eye.

Instead, he asked me a very curious question. "Kirito, in the beta test, you failed to beat the tenth-floor boss, correct?"

"Uh…yeah, that's right. The labyrinth was this traditional Japanese-style place called the Castle of a Thousand Serpents. We only got partway through it."

"And the guild flag did not drop from any more bosses to that point?"

"It didn't…I believe."

"Right," Lind murmured. "So that would mean it's highly likely that situation one cannot happen until at least the tenth floor…"

I nodded. If it dropped on the fifth floor, it seemed like the tenth would be a good bet, but there was no use making guarantees. At this point, I wished that we'd tried a bit harder in the beta and actually beaten the tenth-floor boss, but there was no whining about that now. Besides, the monsters in the Castle of a Thousand Serpents—especially the snake samurai Orochi Elite Guard and the snake ninja Kuchina Elite Assassin—were devastatingly powerful, and just the thought that if we kept going we'd be forced to fight them one day soon sent a chill down my back. I didn't even want to imagine the floor boss who ruled over them.

*Man, I could really go for a cup of hot green tea*, I thought, waiting for him to continue. But Lind did not comment on the feasibility of the second option. He opened his window. I watched his hand movements out of an abundance of caution, but what he brought out was not a weapon but an extremely large leather sack.

He grabbed it off the top of the window and set it down on the low table. It made a heavy, metallic scraping sound.

"There's three hundred thousand col in there," Lind announced to our astonishment. "It's the most the DKB can give you at this moment. Will you sell the guild flag to us at that price?"

Later—much, much later—Asuna would chuckle and say to me, "If you had immediately agreed to sell it, I would've grabbed the bag of money and chucked it through the window."

But in that moment, I stared at the leather sack on the table, unable to respond. I wasn't stunned by the sheer presence of 300,000 in col presented to me, and I wasn't trapped between the options of selling or not selling. No, my mind was swept up in a sudden flash to the past.

It was about a month ago: the evening of December 2, 2022. I remembered the date because it was the day of the first boss-strategy meeting in the first-floor town of Tolbana, and it was the day I met Asuna for the very first time, deep in the labyrinth—though the memory that came to mind was unrelated to either of those events.

Through Argo the Rat, the information agent, someone made an offer to buy my Anneal Blade +6. The offer was for 29,800 col, which was upped to 39,800 a few hours later.

The Anneal Blade had two upgrade attempts left—meaning I'd gotten it to +6 without failing—which made it quite valuable at the time, but at most, it was worth thirty-five thousand. Suspicious, I doubled Argo's silence fee from five hundred col to one thousand, and she revealed that her client was none other than Kibaou. I was even more skeptical after that, but it wasn't until the middle of the first-floor boss battle that I realized Kibaou had been a go-between, too.

The man who was actually attempting to buy the Anneal Blade was Diavel the knight, leader of *SAO*'s first raid party. His idea was not to power himself up, but to power me *down*, allowing him to score the last attack bonus on the boss and cement his position as the leader of the game.

But Illfang the Kobold Lord's attack pattern had changed completely since the beta, and as a former beta tester like me, Diavel fell into a trap set by his own past knowledge and expectations, and he perished.

Despite his outward distance, Kibaou had revered Diavel enough to take on the dirty work of buying someone else's weapon for him in secret. Lind had been his faithful, dedicated party member. They both wanted to take over his position, but their significant discrepancies in ideals led them to start their own guilds, which were now the two biggest in the game.

The 300,000 col on the table now was ten times the sum that Diavel offered for my Anneal Blade. That had to be a coincidence; Lind wouldn't have known about what Diavel was doing in secret. If I ever found myself sharing drinks with Kibaou, I'd have to ask him why he took on that request from Diavel, and what he thought about it…

I emerged from my brief reverie, looked Lind right in the face, and shook my head. "No...I wouldn't sell this for even ten times that much. Besides, the ALS would string me up for doing it, and I mean that literally...Plus, let's be real. You didn't actually think I was going to say yes, did you?"

The guild leader shrugged and said simply, "Not really. But it's important to put it out there. If you were actually willing to sell it, it would be worth it, and if you refuse, I get you on record as saying that you can't be bought with cash."

"Ah, I see what you mean. But if we're talking a hundred times...maybe thirty million col could convince me to— *Huk!*"

I finished my sentence in some strange demihuman dialect thanks to Asuna reaching over with a smug expression and spearing me in the side with her hand. Lind did not react, but both Hafner and Shivata rolled their eyes.

I cleared my throat and got back to the subject at hand. "At any rate, may I conclude that the DKB accept and understand the terms for receiving the item now?"

"Yes...I shall have to acknowledge the current situation as the most reasonable compromise. I do not wish for the standoff between us and the ALS to get worse, either. But after having seen its stats for myself, it's a terrible shame that we can't use the guild flag in the next boss fight."

"I agree. We'll try to think of a way to put it to use, and I'm always looking out for ideas, so send me a message if you think of something."

"Understood."

At that, Lind and Hafner rose to their feet. I was going to watch them go, but then I remembered that it was the DKB who rented this room, so I got up in a hurry.

We filed out of the room in a line, and then Lind turned back toward me. "By the way...are the other inns outfitted with these obnoxious puzzles?"

"Your answer is half yes, half no," I said, grinning. Lind looked skeptical. "I mean, it's not just the inns. The NPC shops, the houses, the other locations...Aside from the front doors, every door to every room in this town has a puzzle on it. So have fun with that."

I patted the stunned brush master on the shoulder and hurried down the stairs.

# 4

"...WELL, THAT WRAPPED UP A LOT QUICKER THAN I thought it would," Asuna said once we were a fair distance away from the Pegasus Hoof. Something in her tone suggested disappointment.

"Are you saying you'd have preferred if we argued over it more...?"

"Of course not, you dummy."

The fencer brandished a fist, then glanced around before continuing in a quieter voice, "I was expecting a more forward-thinking response. It's not like a second flag is going to drop any day now, so the only way for us to make use of it on this floor is the second option, merging—it's obvious to everyone. So I figured, if anyone's going to make the first notions toward that end, it would be the DKB, rather than the ALS..."

"You did? Why do you say that?" I asked, sensing that both sides were more likely to say they'd prefer going to war than joining forces as a single group.

Asuna said, "The ALS is a group pursuing a set of ideals, and the DKB is a group pursuing practical ends. I'm sure there'd be some amount of reshuffling in the event of a merger, of course, but doesn't it seem like the DKB members would complain about it less? It's like they already know they're the true model for tackling this game, and they have the confidence to go along with it..."

"Ahhh…Yeah, I see what you're saying." I looked up at the bottom of the seventh floor, hanging a hundred yards above us.

The Aincrad Liberation Squad was obviously named for the final goal of liberating all ten thousand—well, eight thousand now—players who were trapped in this floating castle. But it also felt like it contained another message: liberation from a status quo where just fifty or sixty elite players monopolized all of the game's resources.

On the other hand, the name of the Dragon Knights Brigade, whoever had thought of it, didn't seem to have much of a meaning. It was the typical kind of fanciful nomenclature you'd find in any online RPG. If changing the guild name was a sticking point in merging the two sides, Asuna was probably right that the DKB members would have less resistance to the idea.

That was why she'd been hoping that the DKB would display an amenability to the idea, giving us a pathway to a possible merger. But…

"The *SAO* system only allows for one guild leader," I muttered. The footsteps next to me came to a stop. I slowed myself down and added, "Even if we could get merger negotiations on the table, neither Lind nor Kibaou would want to give up leadership in the end. Because both of them believe he's the one carrying on in Diavel's footsteps."

"…In that case—!"

I was startled by her vehemence and looked over to my right. Asuna was standing there, her hands clenched into fists, staring down at the eight-inch tiles beneath her feet.

"…In that case, why do they leave all the truly dangerous jobs to you? They squabble over these pointless things like ideas and pride, and they always leave you to pay the tab for them. That's not what a leader does."

It was a statement very similar to what she said in the boss chamber yesterday. And I couldn't give her a response that was any different.

"They're not forcing it onto me. It's because I stuck my neck where it didn't belong that I have the guild flag now. And really, I'm more sorry that I dragged you into all of this…"

After I'd made that point yesterday, Asuna had cried.

But today, she did not. She looked up, her hazel-brown eyes strong and determined. When she spoke, her voice was quiet but solid to its core.

"You can't be that flippant about this anymore. The man in the black poncho attacked you last night because you were preventing him from making the ALS and DKB fight, didn't he? In fact, it's more than that…I'm betting that he wanted to steal the guild flag from you, too. It's the perfect tool for turning the frontline players against one another."

"What…? How would the information be getting out that fast? The only people who knew I had the guild flag at that point were the ones who took part in the boss fight with us, and the main members of the ALS…"

And that was when I put it together. The ALS didn't just have Morte the ax wielder, whom I fought on the third floor. They very likely had other members of the black poncho's PK gang infiltrating their ranks. Which meant the info about the guild flag was being passed right along to them.

The ALS was a bit behind the DKB in terms of member level and equipment stats, and they were trying to make up for it by swelling their ranks. Their practice of having a recruiting team that proactively brought in players who wanted to join the top group was admirable, but it also made the guild vulnerable to infiltration by those with ill intent.

It was occurring to me that it'd be smart to get both guilds' leadership together so I could share info about the existence of this PK gang. I shifted gears from my initial denial. "Actually, you might be right about that. But that just makes it more important that I don't foist the flag off on someone else. I already have a decent idea of how they're doing this, and I've got some experience fighting players from the beta…"

Asuna sucked in a sharp breath but let it out after just a second,

long and slow. Then she turned away—fingers brushing the silver rapier hanging at her left side. "And now that I've learned the basics of dueling from you, I have a duty to fight them as well."

"What?! N-no, that wasn't my point…"

"Well, I've decided!" she declared, letting go of the rapier and jabbing her finger at my chest. Like that, my temporary partner gave me my orders: "Listen up! You're not going to rush off without a word to me again, the way you did when you went searching for Argo on the fourth floor! You must be within my sight for all twenty-four hours. Is that understood?!"

"Whehh?!"

It felt like she was treating me like a preschooler, but Asuna's expression was anything but joking. I opened and shut my mouth a few times to no avail. At last, I protested, "B-but what about when we stay at an inn…?"

To my surprise, Asuna already had an answer for that. Before this point, she'd probably get all red in the face and physically attack me, but now she not only didn't hesitate or stammer, she had an instant response.

"So we'll rent a two-bedroom suite like the last one. If we split the cost, it shouldn't end up being too bad."

"………Ah, r-right…"

I didn't really have any other option.

"Good!" Asuna said like a pleased schoolteacher. She turned on her heel and started walking loudly across the tiles. Within three steps, she stopped and turned back to me again. "Also…where are we going now?"

"Um…"

I looked around. We were on a small path to the east of the central street of Stachion that ran north and south from the teleport square. Although it was a backstreet, it was wide, with a strip of greenery on the right side of the path and a row of tiny shops on the left. Some were restaurants, as evidenced by the fragrant smells tickling my nose.

"......How about we get lunch first, then hit up the lord's mansion?" I suggested.

Asuna agreed, smiling again at last. "Good idea. I'd like to eat something that seems appropriate for the New Year holiday."

"That...might be tough..."

But on the inside, I was running through my memory, trying to remember if the menus of the restaurants here had anything that fit the season.

We had a lunch of meatloaf and shrimp fritters, which might be very generously interpreted as a Western-style take on Japanese *osechi* cuisine for New Year's Day. Then we headed up the gentle staircase road north until we arrived at the mansion that overlooked the rest of Stachion.

Behind the mansion was the outer perimeter of Aincrad itself, so the pale blue expanse was very close at hand. If you turned 180 degrees at the large front gate, you saw the rectangular town before you, followed in the distance by the wilderness of the sixth floor.

"...When you see it all like this, you realize that six miles across really is a huge amount of space..." Asuna remarked. I was about to tell her that Aincrad was cone-shaped, and that each floor was about two hundred feet narrower than the one before, but then I realized it wasn't really important enough to make a big deal over.

"Your typical open-world RPG's map is around six to twelve miles long in each direction, so it's like a bunch of them all stacked atop one another. According to the legend of the Great Separation that Kizmel mentioned, Aincrad was built out of pieces of land cut from the continent below. Makes you wonder how big *that* map must be..."

"...And in the forest elves' legend, collecting the six keys and opening the Sanctuary will return Aincrad to the land," Asuna said. It brought back all the details of the "Elf War" quest's background.

"And the dark elves said that opening the Sanctuary will cause

Aincrad to fall to ruin…right? We definitely want to avoid things getting ruined, but I'd also rather not have it all go back to the earth. What if this map was suddenly dozens or hundreds of times larger? It's hard to stay motivated to keep going that way."

"Wouldn't you be able to skip having to do each and every labyrinth—and just jump straight ahead to the final boss's dungeon?"

"Oh, good point…but there's no way you could beat him…"

For an instant, I started to imagine the final boss waiting on the hundredth floor, as Akihiko Kayaba had said on the first day of our imprisonment. Then I shook my head to dispel the vision.

"C'mon, let's go inside. We'll get the quests from the lord and try to finish all the ones in town by the end of the day."

Cylon, the lord of Stachion, was a small and skinny man who looked simply dreadful in his magnificent beard and flashy toga. He didn't put on airs, however; he was quite welcoming to these strangers who showed up at his door. In fact, we had to wait awhile outside his chamber because there were three groups of players in line already, but that wasn't his fault. They even served us tea.

Cylon's appearance and background story were exactly the same as in the beta, but it was still worth paying attention for a refresher.

According to him, the abundance of puzzles all over the town was the result of a curse placed upon the previous lord.

His name was Pithagrus, and he was a man who loved numbers and puzzles. He bragged day and night that there was no puzzle he could not solve. One day, a traveler visiting his mansion produced an exceedingly complex numerical puzzle, and Pithagrus could not solve it. In his rage, he picked up a nearby golden cube and beat the traveler to death with it. The traveler's last breath was a curse, and ever since then, Stachion was possessed by puzzles of all kinds…

"Pithagrus was driven mad by this, and he left Stachion forever, carrying only the bloodstained golden cube with him. It has been ten years already since then...I suspect he is no longer among the living," Cylon said, sipping his tea dejectedly.

"As Pithagrus's senior apprentice," he continued, "I took on the responsibilities of his office and worked my hardest to undo the curse the murdered traveler enacted, but the puzzles only grow—a new one appears in the town every day. Nearly all the town's interior doors and storage boxes are afflicted by puzzles already, and their front doors will not be long. By that point, it will no longer be possible for us to live here...Good swordsman, please find the golden cube that Pithagrus took from this mansion and bring it back. If the cube is placed on the traveler's grave, and prayers are dedicated to his memory, the curse of the puzzles will surely be undone. Please, please save Stachion from this menace!"

Cylon bowed deeply, causing a golden *!* to appear over his head. Asuna glanced at me and said, "Very well. We accept your request."

It promptly turned into a *?* at that point. Next came the time for questions, but since we knew other players were in line to get their quests, we kept it to a minimum, then scurried out of the guest room. After that, we took a quick tour of the mansion, which was still very video game–like, thanks to its cubic construction. Lastly, we headed out into the backyard to say a quick prayer at the grave of the traveler who'd been killed by the previous lord.

"Ahhh...Going into mansions like that, I always want to just rifle through all the bookshelves and drawers and pots and stuff," I said, stretching my back.

Asuna made an exaggerated show of pulling away in disgust. "Ew...Is that your fetish, Kirito...?"

"What?! F-first of all, it's not a fetish, and second of all, it's an RPG staple that you go around ransacking people's houses for items! Although, in a lot of the Western ones, the guards will chase you if you do..."

For three seconds, Asuna greeted my protestation with an even more suspicious look. Then she burst into giggles. "Well, I suppose you're not the type to go sneaking around and taking stuff.

You'd rather dump out the owner's entire inventory right in front of their face."

"I—I don't recall doing any such…"

Then I remembered when I had Asuna materialize all of her belongings on the second floor, and I suddenly had to clear my throat.

"…thing with malice. My point is, let's get cracking on these quests. The "Curse of Stachion" is a really long quest series, so if we don't do them quickly, we could get left behind at the boss battle. And on top of that, we've got more 'Elf War' quests on this floor."

"I'm more interested in *those*, to be honest. Between all the murdered travelers and missing lords, the local story seems a bit dark."

"As a general rule, RPG quests tend not to be fun and delightful affairs," I commented. But the truth was that I wanted to see Kizmel again as soon as possible. On the other hand, the longer a quest series was, the better the experience bonus you received. High-risk, high-return experience gains were tough to pull off—the last thing anyone wanted was to die—so diligently checking off quests was still the quickest way to level up.

Asuna suddenly tossed her arms into the air and stretched like she was doing morning calisthenics. "Okay, let's do this! Where are we going first?" she exclaimed.

"To an old man who was the butler to the old lord—to ask him questions," I answered. Her excitement meter visibly plummeted.

"Ugh, that's so boring…and we're going to have to wait at the entrance again, aren't we…?"

"Shall we buy some ring puzzles to play with while we wait?"

"No, thanks."

The fencer shook her head sadly and trudged off. I trotted after her.

The former butler's house was at the very southern end of Stachion, completely across town. If the northern half was the luxurious side with its ample greenery, the southern half was the more urban side, with small houses clustered around cramped alleys. Most of the buildings were made of wood—but eight-inch wooden blocks rather than boards and pillars—so they looked more like life-size block houses.

Fortunately, there were no other players at our destination, and we were done talking to the elderly NPC in just over ten minutes and on our way.

His story was the same as it had been in the beta. The former butler wasn't present for the murder of the traveler; he heard the screams and rushed to the master's chamber, only to see the ghastly body. The way he described it, the head was beaten to a pulp, and the humble traveling garb was covered in blood. In the beta, people had muttered, "This quest has to be rated R!"

The butler had no leads on the location of Pithagrus or the golden cube, but rather predictably, he did say that the maidservant at the time might know something. So we headed to the servant's home next.

As we walked the narrow path, Asuna brought up a very reasonable question. "Say...don't you know the final destination for this quest already, Kirito? Couldn't we just skip all these steps and go right there?"

"Actually...you can't. If you don't go in order, things break down. Characters won't talk to you, and events won't happen. If we hadn't talked to Cylon first, that old man back there probably wouldn't have let us into his home."

"...And how many more people do we need to talk to in town, by the way?"

"Six."

She abruptly blurted, *"Falyoon!"*

"...What was that?"

"I was saying, 'I much prefer the generic monster-killing quests to manhunt quests,' in Elvish!"

*"Nga-grunga."*

"...What was that?"

"'I completely agree,' in Orcish."

And on and on, we chatted and joked as we made our way

across Stachion to the home of the maidservant who'd happily married her way out of the job (they didn't actually say that).

From there, we went to the former gardener, then cook, then first apprentice, then second apprentice, then favorite bartender, until at last we got the piece of information that Pithagrus owned a separate home in a neighboring town. That was the end of the questline in Stachion for the moment.

As we left the pub, the sky from the outer aperture was reddish-purple. It was five thirty in the afternoon by then, largely because at a number of these quest stops, the people had errands of their own to do.

Asuna stretched. She looked tired. "So after all that…we didn't learn very much. Pithagrus was an eccentric, but everyone seems to admire him, and he didn't have a wife or children. That was it, I think? And nobody knows who the murdered traveler was—or where they were from…"

"Well, that's not so strange, now, is it? If you're a traveler here, you don't have a passport or social media accounts to follow."

"But the teleporters weren't active ten years ago, so if it's a traveler, they came from somewhere on the sixth floor, right?" she wondered, looking up. "There are maybe three or four other villages here, so if we wanted to track them down, it should be possible to identify them, don't you think…?" At that, she stared straight at *me*.

"Wh-what?"

"Hang on…you know the ending to this quest, don't you? Where did Pithagrus go? Who was the traveler?"

"Um…you're really gonna ask that question?"

Whether it was online multiplayer or not, a game's story was a sensitive area when it came to spoilers. Some people didn't care at all, and some people got furious over it. Survival was the utmost priority in *SAO*, of course, and Asuna didn't seem the type to get hung up on spoilers, but I'd been careful to not reveal the outcome of quests before we got to them.

After a brief look of surprise, Asuna realized what I meant by that and let out a little giggle. "Ohhh, so you've been holding back for my sake! Well, it's all right. I don't get all worked up about this sort of quest."

"Um...*this* sort of quest...? Then what sort of quest *would* you get upset about—over spoilers?"

"The heartwarming ones and the tear-jerking ones."

"......"

Out of all the quests we'd done together, which ones would she classify as heartwarming and which as tear-jerking? And what category did the "Curse of Stachion" fall under? After a few seconds, I came to the conclusion that it was pointless to try to figure it out.

"...Um, so am I correct in thinking that you won't get mad if I tell you the ending of this quest?"

"No worries. It's totally one of the disappointing kinds, right?"

"......"

I hated to admit it, but she was right. After all the trouble I went through to finish it in the beta, I was left with such a bad aftertaste that I wanted a word with the scenario writer.

"Okay, then I'm going to spoil the hell out of it...There was never any traveler to begin with."

"Huh?!" Asuna yelped. She came to a stop and turned toward me. "No traveler...? But the butler and the maidservant saw the body, right? And the gardener dug the hole for the grave in the backyard. So who was it that got killed and buri...? Oh!"

She stopped herself in a moment of epiphany. I gave her a little round of applause.

"Bingo. That was the body of Pithagrus, the former lord. And the one who killed him was..."

"......Cylon?"

"Bingo again. Cylon was the first apprentice of Pithagrus the puzzle king, but when he announced that a different apprentice would take over as his true heir, he got furious and beat his master to death. To hide his crime, he pulverized the face until it was unrecognizable, then put on shabby clothes to transform himself into a made-up traveler..."

"I knew it! I *knew* it!" she shouted abruptly, hands on her hips with her face thrust forward. "I knew it was going to be a disappointing one! That's why I don't like this kind of quest! And what's the 'puzzle king' supposed to mean anyway? What do you get by being the heir to the puzzle king?!"

"D-don't yell at *me*. I didn't write it...I don't know what they get out of it, but there are quiz kings and medal kings and so on. Some people just really want to have that honor, I guess?"

"It doesn't make sense...And for that matter, I don't know what a medal king is supposed to be, either..."

"Sorry, forget I said it. At any rate, that's the ending. But you get a ton of experience for it, so let's just tough it out and beat the quest."

"All right," Asuna said, unconvinced. She looked up at the bottom of the floor above. The lid of rock and steel was turning deep purple, signaling that night would arrive within an hour. The next town over was a mile away, and there wouldn't be many monsters along the road, so we could definitely get there before it was dark, but the problem was the next step after that. Pithagrus's other home was an empty ruin now, and it would be full of astral-type monsters (i.e., ghosts) that we'd have to fight multiple times before we got the next clue. I decided to keep that part a secret, clapping the fencer lightly on the shoulder.

"Let's get dinner in the next town, and then we can continue the quest. If we can finish it up by the end of tomorrow, we should be able to get to the dark elf fortress the day after."

Asuna's face lit up, and she gave me an energetic "Great!"

Suribus, the second town on the sixth floor, was a beautiful place with a southern European air and absolutely no little eight-inch blocks.

A large river running through its middle was spanned by

numerous bridges—a sight that was reminiscent of Rovia, the main town of the fourth floor—though, regrettably, this river had not a single gondola in it. Still, the view of orange lights reflecting off the dark surface of the water had a kind of ethereal beauty you could only find in a virtual world. We had to stop on the bridge leading into the town for a moment to drink it all in.

"...This town doesn't have any cursed puzzles in it, right?" Asuna said right off the bat.

"Nope," I confirmed. "If you want some to go, they sell 'em in the gift shops."

"I don't," she stated firmly. "More importantly, let's get something to eat. What's good in Suribus?"

"Hmm, let me think..."

In the beta, I just ran through the quests and didn't spend much time here, and upon further reflection, there weren't many opportunities to eat in Aincrad back then. If I had time, I wanted to spend it leveling up, and if I got full in the virtual world, my mom and sister would yell at me. I tried to dig through what dim memories I had of the place to little effect.

"It's a wrap bake."

I spun around in alarm at the sound of a voice right behind us, covering Asuna to protect her.

Leaning against the stone railing was not, however, the man in the black poncho who'd tried to kill me the other day; it was a small woman in a sand-brown cape. The top half of her face was hidden behind straw-yellow curls, but there was no mistaking the three whisker markings on either cheek.

This was the best and only source of information in Aincrad, Argo the Rat. She looked stunned for a second, then pouted. "What's this? What'd I do to earn this kind of reaction from you, Kii-boy? That hurts."

"S-sorry...I'm kind of on edge right now. It's Sneak Attack Caution Week, let's call it..."

Asuna popped out from behind my back. "Good evening,

Argo! I didn't see you in Stachion—of course, you must've been over here already."

"Evenin', A-chan." Argo waved at her and pushed herself off the railing to walk closer. "Well, I'd like ta get my first strategy guide out by tomorrow, but it looks like most of the front-runners are already moving from the main town here to Suribus."

"Oh, they are? But why—?" I started to ask before the reason occurred to me. "Oh…It's because the puzzles are a pain in the ass…isn't it?"

"Hee-hee-hee! Bingo. And the monsters aren't too tough around these parts…so while I hate ta be the bearer of bad news, just about all the rooms in Suribus are booked. Only the expensive suites are available."

Asuna and I glanced at each other. We'd been planning to stay in a suite with two bedrooms tonight anyway, so the single rooms being taken wasn't a problem. But given Argo's rather menacing motto of "selling any info that can be sold," this free tip was a bit—no, make that *very*—suspicious.

"Ohhh, I s-see. But I'm sure that if we look, we can find an open room or two," I replied. Argo's eyebrow twitched, but she said nothing more on the matter.

"Welp…based on what you were sayin' earlier, I'm guessin' you two are about to eat dinner?"

"Yes, we were just deciding what to have," Asuna said. "Argo, you said this town was famous for its wrap bakes? Do you have a recommended restaurant?"

"I just made my way over here from Stachion earlier today, actually. Only had a chance to try out one place, but it was mighty tasty."

"Then let's go to that one!" Asuna insisted. Argo had no choice but to grimace and go along with it. If it was me, she'd have demanded a price for that intel, but now that Asuna had identified her as a good friend, the Rat seemed unable to inflict her usual business practices.

Argo took us to a place on the third floor of a building along the river that ran through Suribus. It was kind of a hidden, hole-in-the-wall type establishment. The first and second floor were just homes, and there was no sign, so you weren't likely to find it unless you knew about it already.

The stairs were narrow enough you could barely go two ways on them, and the door at the end was faded and marked with knots, but the interior of the place was quite clean. There was a counter and two tables for four, so we took one of them.

I was imagining that the famous "wrap bake" would be something like *gyoza* dumplings, but what came out was essentially a round meat pie about eight inches across. Meat, tomato-flavored veggies, and plenty of cheese were all wrapped in a hot crispy crust. It wasn't bad. In fact, it was great.

In a blink, I'd reduced the circle pie to a semicircle. I took a long drink of cold herbal tea, then asked the info dealer, "Are all the wrap bakes in this town the same tomato-and-cheese flavor?"

"Nope. If it's like it was in the beta, each place will serve a different kind. Since it's a riverside town, most of 'em were fish."

"Fish pie...? Seems weird to me..." I murmured.

But Asuna had a huge grin on her face. "Just like the famous herring and pumpkin pie, I suppose."

"F-famous...?"

I craned my head back the other way, wondering if there was such a staple dish in Aincrad, and saw that Argo was smirking as well. "A-chan, if you're going to make a reference a game addict is going to understand, it has to be from a game."

"I suppose you're right..."

"You've got a lot of work ahead of you in your future..."

"No kidding...I m-mean, not that I've decided this partnership is lasting forever!"

"Nee-hee-hee-hee!"

In the moment, I had the feeling that although it was hard to tell what exactly they were talking about, it was probably better that I didn't know, so I returned my attention to the half-finished meat pie.

Now that I thought of it, this might have been the first time I'd ever tasted a truly orthodox tomato flavor in Aincrad. Food in this world tended to be light on flavoring but heavy on spice. It was good once you got used to it, but most restaurants had one little thing—or sometimes a big thing—that felt unsatisfying afterward.

This pleasantly overdone tomato flavor, however, was almost reminiscent of junk food to me. I'd have loved to try it heaped on top of soft-boiled spaghetti rather than in a neat little pie…but I still finished every last bite of the meal anyway.

"Ahhhh…Nice work, Argo. You know the best places to go."

"Don't I? Now, I'm not sayin' ya owe me for the tip, but…"

She looked around the room, ensuring there were no other players present, then whispered, "The big thing…How'd it all turn out?"

Given that we were alone, it seemed like she could have just said the name of the item in question. But it was an important enough topic that I couldn't get touchy about it.

I leaned over the table and whispered, quiet enough that no Eavesdropping skill could pick it up through the door, "We gave the DKB the same conditions we did to the ALS. They did accept our terms, but…"

"But?"

"They also tried to buy it off us for three hundred thousand col."

Argo blinked once, very slowly. Her painted-on whiskers twitched. "Heh-heh. So that's their tactic. Well, in that case…"

"…*He really is takin' over for Diavel*," she left unsaid, downing the rest of her herb tea. Asuna looked at us for answers, but I whispered "I'll explain later" before getting us back to the topic at hand.

"At any rate, it looks like I'll be holding on to it for the time being. The only problem is: That means we can't use it for this upcoming boss fight…so they were on the same page in hoping to find a shortcut to it."

"A shortcut, huh…?" Argo folded her arms and murmured to

herself. Then she grinned again. "Remember what the chakram guy who helped you with the fifth-floor boss said? If you started up a guild, all the Legend Braves would join ya. In fact, if ya made A-chan the leader instead of yerself, I bet you'd have a whole crowd o' folks lookin' to join. How about that?"

"Wh...what?"

Just this morning, Asuna had said she didn't want to be the subleader of a guild. She shook her head back and forth so violently that the ends of her long hair smacked me in the face.

"Y-you've got to be joking! It's annoying enough for me to watch after him. I want nothing to do with any guild master job!"

"A-annoying...?"

I wasn't expecting that her answer was going to throw *me* under the bus. Argo just chuckled to herself.

We said good-bye to the info dealer outside the meat-pie place and headed right for Pithagrus's other home on the edge of town.

The river running through Suribus was flowing from a waterfall that emerged directly from one of the massive pillars at the outer aperture of Aincrad, and it continued through to the lake in the center of the floor. The town was built in a narrow strip along both banks of the river, with countless bridges crossing back and forth. Some of those bridges actually had full buildings on top of them, with roofs and everything. One of these "bridge houses" was our quest destination.

We started this day training in the dark elf camp on the third floor, then talked with the DKB, followed by running all over town doing quests, leaving town and fighting our first monsters in the evening, and now reaching Suribus for dinner. Naturally, Asuna was looking a bit fatigued, but as soon as she saw the bridge where we were heading, her eyes lit up.

"Ooh, it's lovely! Just like the Ponte Vecchio!"

The name sounded familiar to me, so I consulted my memories of the real world—in danger of being entirely overwritten by that of this fantasy realm—and asked, "Erm, are you talking about... the bridge in that, er...famous Tokyo theme park...?"

Asuna blinked twice, then smiled. "Ah, right. They copied it there, too, didn't they? In the water park, not the land one. But the original Ponte Vecchio is a bridge in Florence, Italy, spanning the Arno River. The real one's much bigger than this one, of course, but it's just as beautiful…"

She looked up at the bridge house again, enchanted, while I fell into my thoughts. This was now the second time (ever since the fourth floor) my temporary partner had mentioned the name of a city in Italy. At this point, it was probably a good bet that she'd actually been there herself—not just read about it. That on its own wasn't important, but it did fit a pattern, combined with her looks, communication skills, lack of gaming knowledge, and richness of *other* knowledge, that suggested Asuna had an extremely fulfilling and "normal" life in the real world. So how did she wind up logging into *SAO* on the very first day, when only ten thousand copies had been shipped (and nine thousand turned on), getting herself stuck in here…?

"C'mon, let's get going! I bet the river is gorgeous from up there!"

She patted me on the back, and I returned to my senses.

"Oh, y-yeah, I bet…"

From the outside, Pithagrus's second mansion was pretty, but it was a total wreck on the inside. It was also full of ghost-type monsters, which Asuna described as "not my forte"—which probably meant she was completely terrified of them. But before I could explain any of that, the fencer had marched off for the building, and the only thing I could do was chase after her.

As we traveled along the river toward the bridge, three players were descending the stone stairs that led up to the house over the water. On instinct, we stopped behind the trees lining the road and listened to them speak.

"…No way that door opens…"

"Waste of time. Forget this whole thing. Three digits is bad enough, but six is impossible!"

"Yeah, I just feel like there's gotta be something good in there..."

The grumbling trio passed by our position and left. From the tree next to mine, Asuna gave me a sidelong glance.

"...Is there another puzzle door?"

"...Yes."

"...You said they were only in the main town."

"N-no, it's just the one here...I think," I added, stepping back into the street.

The bridge that Asuna compared to Ponte Vecchio was about eighty feet long and twenty feet wide. The first story was just a normal bridge, but the side railings were dotted with pillars that formed countless arches supporting the living space on the second story. After having spent so much time in Stachion with its uniform, blocky look, the structure here was, indeed, elegant and attractive.

At the edge of the railing were especially large supports—the main pillars, as they called them—the sort that often featured a plaque with the bridge's name on it. One had a short staircase attached to it that led up to Pithagrus's house over the bridge itself. As I approached the old door, I couldn't help but reflect that games taught you to *want* to head up little paths like this.

On the surface of the stout wooden door was a six-part metal dial. It was a familiar locking device, where each wheel could turn through all the digits from zero to nine.

Asuna reached it first and tried it out, the dials clicking as she moved the numbers. She turned to me. "None of the quests so far had anyone tell us the key for a numerical lock, did they...? Are we supposed to solve this on our own?"

"You might guess a three-digit code, but six makes it just about impossible. It can be anything from zero to nine hundred ninety-nine thousand, nine hundred ninety-nine, so that's a hundred thousand possibilities..."

"You mean a million."

"Huh? Oh...y-yeah, duh. A million possibilities. So even if you just ran through each and every one, it would take you several days. But, spoiler alert, you can find the correct combination in Cylon's office."

"What? Where was it written?"

"In the landscape painting on the wall," I said.

Asuna's cheeks promptly puffed up. "Hey, you could have said something. If I'd known there would be a hint there, I would have looked closer and spotted it."

"No, I very much doubt that. The way it works is that you're supposed to come here and think, 'I don't know the numbers!' Then you go back to Stachion to ask Cylon, who won't tell you, *but* he makes an odd show of trying to hide the painting. So then he kicks you out and you have to wait for him to leave before you can go back in to search the painting. It's a huge pain…"

"…You're right, I'd rather not go through all that," Asuna admitted. Then her brows knitted again. "But…how does that make sense? I mean, Cylon's the—"

I had a feeling she would blurt this out at some point, so I glanced over my shoulder and cut her off. "We can talk inside. I don't want anyone to see us opening the door."

"Fine, fine, whatever you say. So…what's the correct combination?"

"Let's see…"

I started to answer according to my recollection from the beta, but my spine ran cold. If they had changed the combination between then and the release of the game, I was about to look extremely stupid. Hesitantly, I uttered the six digits.

"…Six, two, eight, four, nine, six."

"Uh-huh…"

She quickly spun the little dials into place. With a very clear *click!* the lock was undone. I stepped forward, relieved, but Asuna just stared at the dials without turning the doorknob.

"What's up? If you don't open it soon enough, the lock will engage again."

"Oh…y-yeah. I was just thinking, the numbers seemed familiar somehow. Maybe I really did spot them in the painting without realizing it," she said vaguely as she opened the door. It was pitch-black inside, and a draft of chilly, damp air swept outward. The fencer fell back on her heels a bit, sensing something foreboding, but I grabbed her shoulders from behind and kept her moving forward.

Once we were inside, the door shut behind us on its own. There was a scraping sound, which was just the number dials from the lock shuffling themselves again, but I felt Asuna's shoulders jump under my fingers.

"…Um, it's dark in here."

"Yeah, it's night."

"…How are we going to search the place like this? Should we wait until the morning and come back?"

"No, we're fine."

I opened up my window and materialized an item that I always had on the first page of my inventory.

"*Laaanterrrn*," I said in a spooky voice, hoping this would lighten up the mood. All I got was a cold stare over Asuna's shoulder. I cleared my throat awkwardly and lit the device, filling the area with orange light.

As one might expect from a home belonging to the lord of Stachion, the entrance hall was quite spacious. Because it was built on top of a bridge, it was inevitably a bit elongated and narrow in shape, but the hallway that ran down the left wall was plenty wide enough not to feel cramped.

On the other hand, there were bundles of cobwebs in the corners of the ceiling, and broken utensils and torn pieces of paper were all over the floor. It very much had the appearance of an abandoned house. The look on Asuna's face said this wasn't what she signed up for.

She turned to me. "So…back to what I was saying."

"What was that…? Oh, about Cylon?"

"Yes. Does what he's doing make any sense? If he's the one who killed Pithagrus and buried the body in traveler's garb in the backyard, why is he asking us to investigate the incident for him?"

"Nuh-uh. Cylon didn't ask us to investigate the killing of the traveler. He asked us to look for the golden cube that was used in the murder."

"Oh, right…" The small furrow between her eyebrows eased for a moment, then returned. "No, but that still doesn't make sense. Cylon was the one who beat Pithagrus to death with the golden cube, right? So wouldn't Cylon have hidden the weapon?"

"Well, the reasoning behind that comes up at the end of the quest…but whatever. So Cylon got mad and beat Pithagrus to death, then mocked him up into a traveler who didn't exist to hide his crime, right? He thought it all worked out in the end, but somehow the cube vanished from the murder scene—a cube with Cylon's bloody fingerprints on it. On top of that, it's the town treasure and the symbol of its lord—the very cube that formed the sizing basis of all the stone and wood cubes that make up the town. So Cylon's idea is that the only way to purify the puzzle curse upon Stachion is to find the missing cube, clean off his prints, then place it at the grave of the traveler…who is secretly Pithagrus himself."

"……It just seems…very selfish. Or convenient. If he really wanted to undo the puzzle curse, he shouldn't be bothering with the cube. He should admit that he killed Pithagrus and turn himself in to the police, right?"

"Well, yeah. But there are no police in Aincrad."

Asuna murmured a soft "Oh yeah," but her indignation still remained. She brought up the town guards, the dark elf fortress, even Blackiron Palace down in the Town of Beginnings on the first floor as a list of places he where he could turn himself in to a higher authority.

"…Well?" she finished, looking at me.

"Well…what?"

"What do you think I mean? Who stole the golden cube? You're not going to tell me it grew arms and legs of its own and ran away……Oh!"

"'Oh'…what?"

"Is that actually what it is? You said the boss of this floor is like a giant Rubik's Cube. Did the golden cube turn into some kind of monster form?"

Now it was my turn to be stunned. As impressed as I was with the fencer's imagination, I had to shake my head.

"Sadly, that is not the case. Actually, maybe it's not sad—if that boss cube were completely gold, you'd have no idea how to rotate it to solve the sides. But back to the point…we've already met the person who removed the cube."

"Whaaat?" She scowled, then let her eyes wander as she considered this. "So you're saying…it's one of the seven people we talked to in Stachion? The former butler, the maidservant, the gardener, the cook, the two apprentices, and the bartender he liked to visit…? And one of them has the cube now? Who is it?"

"Let's find that out on our own. We're here to get the clues, after all," I said with an evil grin.

She pouted. "Fine, let's get on with it. You know which room has the clue in it, right?"

"Sadly, the place where the key item pops up is randomized."

"…So we'll just have to start with the first room and go in order."

The swordswoman started walking down the entrance hall. As she went, I called out, "Oh, and a few of the rooms have ghosts, so don't forget to prepare for battle."

"Sure, sure, whatever."

*Step-step-step, pause.*

All of a sudden, she had teleported behind my back with her hands on my shoulders. An unyielding force pushed me on toward the first room.

Fortunately, like in the beta, there was no dial lock on the inside doors. I pushed it open to a room that was actually darker than the hallway. Even with the lantern held up, the light didn't reach all the corners of the room.

"…Was there a ghost?" came a tiny voice behind my back. For the briefest of moments, my penchant for mischief kicked in, but

I knew that playing pranks here would be the end of our partnership, so I gave her an honest answer.

"Doesn't seem like there's one in this room."

"I don't want *seems*! I want it on the record!"

"Fine, fine. There are no ghosts in here."

At last, Asuna emerged from hiding behind my back, looking as smug and in control as ever as she inspected the room. "Ew... it's in a terrible state..."

I had to concur. It was probably a guest parlor originally, with a deluxe set of furniture in the middle of the moderate-sized room, and a huge fireplace on the far wall. But all the other furniture had collapsed after ten years of disuse, and the carpet was eaten through by insects.

Asuna approached a side table that was still intact and ran a finger across its surface, which was piled high with dust. She made another face. "This was probably luxury furniture at one point. Not much use for it anymore..."

"Well, you might be able to refurbish it if you take it to an NPC woodworker."

"Wait, you can do that? I thought you couldn't move the objects in an NPC's home."

"As a general rule. But in these safe-zone dungeons, there are a fair number of furniture pieces whose coordinates aren't locked," I explained, moving next to Asuna and grabbing the side table with both hands. When I pulled upward, the legs came right off the ground.

"There, you see?"

"You're right...Hmm. But even if it got fixed up, I don't think I'd want to use furniture that came from a place like this. For one thing, I have no idea when I might ever have a place of my own."

"Yeah, that's a good point," I said, lowering the table. But that vibration, as tiny as it was, managed to do in its remaining durability, and it crumbled pathetically into a pile of wood.

"Ooooh, you busted it—you're in trouble!" Asuna teased me, grinning wolfishly. She leaned onto the back of a nearby three-seat sofa, and instantly, the legs cracked off. It finished its act by split-ting in two, through both the seat and the back portion.

"Ooh, I'm gonna tell the teacher!" I taunted back, which I didn't think I'd said even when I was actually in elementary school. Asuna snorted and grinded her left fist against my side. I couldn't very well return that jab, and it left me helpless to do anything but grind my teeth in frustration.

"There doesn't seem to be anything else here. Let's go to the next one," I said, pointing at the door.

"Fine, if you say so…but what are we even looking for anyway?"

"Something that would suggest the location of the golden cube."

"And what is that something…? Well, if it's the key to this quest, I bet they'll make sure it's visible one way or another."

"Let's hope so…" I said knowingly as I headed into the hall-way. I checked the front door just in case, but it didn't seem to have been opened while we were in the parlor. Asuna checked the same direction and seemed to notice something, however.

"Hey…what happens if someone else solves the combination on the dials while we're already in here?"

"It's not an instanced location. So they'd come right in here."

"…And what happens if that person finds the clue item before we do?"

"I'd say that the item would be locked in place so you can't move or destroy it, or it would be something you could find infi-nitely. But in the latter case, it would spawn at certain intervals. There are some that take thirty minutes or an hour to reappear. Some even last as long as a day before they come back…"

"Then we'd better find it and get out of here. C'mon, next, next!"

Asuna pushed me several steps down the hallway until we came to a new door.

The room adjacent to the parlor was a large dining room. The massive dinner table and chairs were still intact, but the way that ten or so table settings with cutlery included were laid out on top was quite eerie. The wine bottles and candleholders were gray with dust, and the chandelier hanging from the ceiling supported many spiderwebs.

For five seconds, Asuna cowered behind my back. Once she was certain there were no ghosts here, she emerged as if nothing had just happened.

"Can you move the wine and utensils, too?" she asked.

"Probably. You wanna take that back and drink it?"

"No, thank you. On the other hand, the clue item doesn't seem to be here, either," she murmured. Asuna strode closer to the dining table.

Just then, there was a whooshing, rustling sound like the kind we heard in the underground chapel on the fifth floor, and a pale light spilled out from beneath the table. Passing up through the filthy tablecloth were two astral monsters—based on the long, slim silhouettes and tattered white dresses, they seemed to be wraiths. There were other kinds in this category—specters, phantoms, spirits, apparitions—but I honestly had no idea what differentiated them all.

While she didn't scream the way she had on the floor below, Asuna leaped upward a foot or so and ran through the air—at least it seemed that way to me because she was moving so fast—and darted around behind my back again.

"Th-there they are! Hurry! Do something!" she ordered. I drew my Sword of Eventide +3, but rather than immediately attacking, I kept the wraiths at bay with the tip.

"Asuna, I think it's for the best if you experience some battle against astral types right here."

"B-but..."

"It's all right. You might have forgotten, but we're in town now. No matter how much they attack, you won't lose a single pixel of HP."

*That's not the problem,* she seemed to say with her resulting sigh. But Asuna had thoughts of her own on this, and she peered around my left shoulder. While she immediately shrank back first, she then sidled her entire body until she was at my side instead. With her lantern held high in her off-hand, she drew the Chivalric Rapier +7 and pointed it at the wraiths situated atop the table.

I focused on the ghosts myself, bringing up the automatic cursor. Beneath the HP bar, it said ANNOYING WRAITH in English, and the cursor itself was a very faint pink color. That meant that even if we weren't in town, they wouldn't be tough foes.

"...I don't recall seeing any 'Annoying' Wraiths before," Asuna said, her voice a bit hoarse.

As calmly as I could, I asked her, "What's *anoing* mean?"

"You didn't learn that in English class? It's, like, irritating—or troublesome..."

"Ahh. That would fit for a quest event like this. Like I said, we're in town, so we won't lose any HP. But aside from that, these are the same as any ordinary wraith, so hitting their limbs or the end of their dresses won't do much damage, and if they hit you, they can debuff you."

"Wait...you never warned me about that!" Asuna shrieked, and the wraiths seemed to react to the sound. They spread their arms and descended with a wail: "*Hyoooo!*"

Human-type astral monsters could be male, female, or indeterminate, but wraiths were mostly female, it seemed. However, they had no beauty whatsoever; the arms extending from their ragged dresses were thin as bones, and two-thirds of their faces were skeletal. Blue fires burned in the eye sockets of these ones, and they swung long hands with knife-sharp nails.

I evaded the first attack and swiped at the torso. The deep cut produced a white substance like smoke, but it left little impact, and the wraith only lost a tenth of its health bar.

But the creature screeched hideously and flew to the corner of the dining room. I kept my sword pointed in its direction and glanced over to check on Asuna.

"Why, you! Fngh! Shwaaa!" the fencer was hissing, not to be outdone by the wraiths' bizarre vocalizations. She executed thrust skills with incredible speed—their frequency so thick that even the ghost couldn't get past her rapier. As the wraith flew around in a figure-eight pattern, she occasionally clipped an arm, but it didn't do much HP damage.

Astral types had insubstantial bodies, and regular weapons did not inflict effective damage on them. Other games would have flame or light spells that could wreak havoc on them, but because of the ancient Great Separation of Aincrad, true magic had been lost here. You just had to make do with physical attacks, one way or another.

The most common method was to place a blessing buff on your weapon, but at the moment, that could only be done in large towns with a church, and it cost money. You could also use sword skills with a high anti-astral effect (most of which were mace or flail skills) or bring many illumination items (astral monsters' natural resistance was lower in the light), but these were tough requirements for a group of just two sword users.

Fortunately, both Asuna's Chivalric Rapier and my Sword of Eventide had received elven upkeep, which gave them minor effectiveness against the undead—enough to be good on its own against weak event monsters like these. I thrust my lantern forward and closed the gap so I could take my target out. In this situation, a fighter who used a shield or a two-handed weapon would just have to put the light on the ground to fight, but having a free hand meant I could just hold the lantern. And to get even more into the fine details, not only did having a light equipped in battle help with attacking power, a torch was better because it didn't count as irregular equipment—and it had extra power against an astral foe weak to fire—with the only drawback being that you had to be careful swinging it around indoors, lest you accidentally burn something that could be destroyed.

Lit by the yellow light of the lantern, the Annoying Wraith let out a high-pitched wail and slid to the right to get away. But that was just what I wanted; when it got into range, I used the three-part skill Sharp Nail on it.

The strongest sword skills I had at the moment were the

four-parters Horizontal Square and Vertical Square, which unlocked at proficiency level 150, but they were too wide-ranging for an indoor environment like this. If push came to shove, I couldn't bother myself about not destroying the walls or furniture, but since this was in an anti-crime code area, and there were plenty of unbreakable objects around, I didn't want to have my sword bounce off an obstacle and lose my skill combo.

Sharp Nail, however, was a nice, compact trio of strikes with the same high-angle path. My silver-glowing sword sank into the torso of the Annoying Wraith without catching on the wall or ceiling.

The first and second hits took it down to about a third of its health, but the last one seemed unlikely to finish the job.

Yet, the moment the third erupted, the tip of the Sword of Eventide actually veered away, as if drawn by a magnet. It sliced the wraith's shoulder, passed expertly through the center of the chest, then emerged out the side. Unlike the first two slices, this one came with the sensation of something small and hard breaking.

Counter to my expectations, the wraith's HP bar sank into the red zone and did not stop until it reached zero. The three visual slicing marks hung in the air like some fierce beast's claws, overlapped by the usual blue bursting effect of any dying monster.

I stared at the blade of my second-generation sword, still in the pose with which I finished the swing.

That magnetic sensation I'd gotten was undoubtedly the aiming-adjustment system that the Accuracy boost had given my weapon. I'd thought the effect only kicked in when you intentionally aimed at a weak point, but I had no idea that a wraith-type monster had a little solid nodule in its chest as a vital area, so that meant the Sword of Eventide had basically hit the Annoying Wraith right in that spot of its own volition.

"...Is that true?" I asked it in a tiny voice. The sword didn't reply, of course.

What I did hear, instead, was my partner screaming.

"Uniiiieee!"

It was probably an expression of disgust and frustration. I

turned to see, on the other side of the large dining room, the fencer utilizing a sword skill. It was the best move she had at the moment, Triangular.

A clean hit from that skill, with the power of the Chivalric Rapier +7, would be enough to take out half my HP. It riddled the wraith with near-invisible speed. But the enemy rose right before the skill executed, meaning it only hit the trailing skirt portion. That ectoplasmic white smoke tattered in its wake, but it left the HP bar with 30 percent remaining.

"Hoh-hoh-hooohhh..." the wraith cried—somewhere between a scream and a mocking laugh—and swung its long arms at Asuna as she waited to recover from the skill delay. It didn't do any damage, but Asuna's HP bar lit up with an icon of a pale hand. That was the Chillness debuff that lowered body temperatures uncomfortably.

"Fyah!" Asuna raged, leaping back as soon as she could move again. Despite valiantly holding her sword aloft, her shivering was apparent. Chill did no actual damage, but it was a major annoyance, causing sneezes in battle and keeping you from dodging the enemy's attack.

I rushed up behind her and called out, "Asuna, want h...?"

"No!" she snapped, refusing my aid. She was not entirely going to handle it on her own, however. "Just give me a hint or something! Its HP refuses to go down!"

"Oh...yeah, rapier thrusts are just about the worst kind of attack to use against astrals..."

The Annoying Wraith floating up near the ceiling couldn't have understood what I was saying, but it chose a very appropriate moment to chuckle.

"Asuna, have you mastered any of the slicing kind of sword skills?" I asked.

My partner's voice was hard—surely due to her struggle to control the cold and not because she was actually mad at me—as she replied, "When I reached proficiency one hundred fifty a while back, I learned to use one called Folium."

"Yeah, I guess that would work. Okay, next time the wraith approaches, use Folium right at the middle of its chest."

"Wh…which part is the middle?" she yelled back. I didn't have any immediate answers. Against kobolds or reptoids, I'd tell her "*Where the heart is*"; all humanoids, including players, had hearts (critical points) located just to the left of the center of the chest. Yet, the little nodule I felt in the wraith's chest had been directly in the middle. There was no other way to define it.

"Um…"

I put the sword behind my back and looked around, then picked up a dusty dessert knife off the dining table. It had almost no value as a weapon, and I didn't have the Throwing Knives skill, so it wasn't going to do any real damage, but…

"Yah!"

I tossed the knife, concentrating only on Accuracy, and it landed in the middle of the swaying wraith's chest, right where the little nodule would be, doing just a single pixel of damage to its HP bar before falling to the floor. A red damage effect appeared for just a few scant seconds on the tattered white dress.

"There!" I shouted, but Asuna was already on the move. The wraith floated down from the ceiling as she approached.

Asuna had learned the Annoying Wraith's "path of least resistance" evasion methods from her previous experience and kept the rapier at her side, luring the enemy in as close as possible. The wraith's arms, mostly bone, reached out to grab her again, and a lime-green light burst into being.

The sword skill Folium was a rare slashing attack for the rapier category, but its trajectory was an unorthodox one. It curved upward from the left hip, then jutted into a sharp loop at its peak and ended at the lower right, much like a lowercase cursive *l*. The intention was to deflect the enemy's attack before giving them a counter, but it wasn't suited for hitting a specific point.

Or so I thought.

"*Teyaa!*" The Chivalric Rapier entered the wraith's right side to perfectly pin the point I'd indicated—before doing a loop and exiting out the left flank. It must've broken the tiny weak point, because the third of its HP bar that remained drained all the way to the left edge. The Annoying Wraith let out a hideous wail and burst.

My partner straightened up without a word and returned her sword to its sheath.

I strolled up to her. "Yo, nice control. Did your Accuracy boost kick in just now? Or was that…?"

"*Pah-choo!*" she answered by way of sneezing. She let go of the rapier and wrapped her body in her arms, her face pale. "I…I'm so cold."

"Yeah, you took a Chill effect…I think it wears off after five minutes, so you've just gotta…"

"*Pah-choo!*"

Her second sneeze drowned out the words *tough it out*. Even knowing it was essentially harmless, I couldn't help but pity her paleness and shivering.

At the very end of the beta, we started getting Purify Crystals that could instantly undo multiple debuffs, including this one, but here on the sixth floor, crystals were just starting to become droppable and were still very rare. The only other way to undo the effects would be the individual method for each one—antidote potions for poison, undoing a curse at the church, etc.

Chill had its own special recovery method, of course. You could warm up by the fire, but lanterns and torches didn't put off enough heat. On the other hand, there was that fireplace in the previous room—it occurred to me that it had been put there by design so you could undo the ghosts' effects—but it would be a bit of a pain in the ass. No, a major pain in the ass.

Instead, I opened my window to test out a convenient but somewhat embarrassing method. With both hands, I removed a thick blanket for camping and draped it over my back like a cape. To cover up the embarrassment of what I was about to do, I focused on thoughts like *These long-haired cattle blankets sure are heavy,* and *I could really use a down-filled bedroll by now,* and *I bet that would be expensive.* When I reached Asuna, who looked at me in surprise, I said, "Pardon me" and drew her closer so I could wrap us both up under the blanket.

Instantly, her body froze like a rod between my arms, and right at my ear, her high-pitched, hoarse voice said, "Hey, wh-what are you...doi...? *Pah-choo!*"

"This is the quickest way to undo the Chill effect. Just put up with it for another twenty seconds."

The icy chill from her body started seeping into me, making my nose itch. The chill was just a virtual skin sensation created by the NerveGear, and my real body would be in some hospital room with perfectly controlled temperature at the moment, but I couldn't help but wonder if sneezing here was also prompting a sneeze out there...

"L-listen, even if this is supposed to help undo the debuff, if someone sees us like this, they're going to get the wrong *fwuh...*"

Right at the moment that she trailed off with that odd sound, the chill trickling from her body into mine suddenly vanished. I'd experienced that before: When the Chill effect wore off, it left the body feeling pleasantly warm. It was like the feeling of taking off your clothes in a changing room in the winter, only to sink right into a tub full of delightfully hot water. I couldn't blame her for letting out an odd moan.

She stared at nothing, mind out of focus, until she snapped back to attention, eyes blinking rapidly, and ducked out of my arms.

"Um, that wasn't...It's not..." she babbled, mouth working furiously, and then spun away from me. "W-well...I'm grateful to you for undoing the debuff. But next time, I'd appreciate an explanation first!"

"I figured if I had to describe it first, it would be twice as embarrassing," I said, putting the heavy blanket back into storage.

To my surprise, Asuna said, "Why, that sounds like you've done it before."

"Huh?! W-well, I knew about it because I'd done it in the

beta, of course...but let me be very clear that the other person was like Wolfgang from the Bro Squad but twice as hairy and super-macho, okay?"

"...I don't know if I wish I could've seen that or not," the fencer said, a very strange and subtle smile on her lips. At least her mood had improved. She walked around the dining room, examining the table and the paintings on the wall, but found nothing.

"Well, that made our battle against the ghosts meaningless."

"Hey, that's just how quests go," I bantered back, now that our usual mood had returned. We left the dining room and returned to the hallway.

Between the kitchen, the study, and the bedroom, we defeated four more Annoying Wraiths but still had not found the key item. At last, we were at the final door. Asuna grabbed the doorknob, then side-eyed me.

"Kirito, you didn't know ahead of time that we weren't going to find anything in the first five rooms, did you?"

"I...I don't know how I could have. Like I said, the item would pop in any of the six rooms at random in the beta. I'm...sure that's what happened just now, too."

"You said that like an NPC," Asuna accused, which was an odd thing to say. She opened the door, and a musty smell stung my nostrils.

I recalled that the last door led to a storeroom. I followed Asuna inside, holding my lantern up. It was the smallest of the six rooms, full of wooden shelves lined with wooden boxes, pots, and various items of all sorts.

"Ugh...do we have to open up all these things to search?"

"I'd rather not do that, either," I mumbled, passing through the maze of standing shelves to the back of the room. At the very end, there was a small writing desk along the wall, and sitting atop it, seemingly abandoned in a very meaningful way, was an object that dully reflected the glow of the lantern.

It was a large key, sitting under ten years of dust.

"Oh! That must be it!" Asuna exclaimed eagerly, trotting up

to the desk. I tried to grab her shoulder, but my hand closed on nothing but empty air.

"Asuna, your feet!" I shouted, right as a cracking sound went off under her foot. In the wavering light of the lantern, I saw an old, faded bone.

Asuna froze in a very unnatural position, right as the boss encounter ghost of this haunted house quest emerged from the wall behind the desk.

Unlike the previous wraiths, this Resentful Wraith was male. Once again, my English skill wasn't quite up to the task of informing me what the word *resentful* meant.

The tall, gaunt ghost wore a sweeping, tattered robe like the ancient Romans did, brandishing its freakishly long nails and opening its mouth wide enough that the jaw seemed dislocated so that it could scream, "*Byoouuu!!*"

As I reached for the sword over my back, it occurred to me that the situation wasn't great.

The Resentful Wraith couldn't take down our HP, of course, but it had a wide variety of debuffs, and if we suffered all of them at once, it would take quite some time to recover. That wasn't the worst thing in the world, but I was also afraid of losing the progress we'd made against the wraiths in conquering Asuna's fear of ghosts. I wanted to keep its attention focused on me, but with hardly four feet of space between the stone wall on the left and wooden shelves on the right, there was barely room to swing my sword, much less switch spots with Asuna.

"Asuna, regroup in the hallway!" I shouted, reaching out for her shoulder again. But before I made contact, I heard her voice, much firmer than I would have expected it to be:

"Kirito, can I break the bones on the floor?!"

"Oh...uh, I think those are just there to be spooky."

"Got it!" she shouted, taking a stance that scattered the bones below. She drew her rapier and thrust a series of five jabs with tip-blurring speed at the approaching Resentful Wraith. They were all aimed at the center of its chest, and while the first four

did not have much effect, the fifth one did take a good 15 percent of its HP bar down. The elven blade had scratched the weak point, which must've been in the same place as the earlier enemies'.

"*Byaaaaa!!*" the spirit shrieked with rage, rising up to the ceiling. It began a bewitching technique utilizing a figure-eight motion, but without the space of the dining room, its side-to-side movement was limited. Relieved, I realized that this would make it easier for the rapier to aim at the spots where it was floating, letting us take down its HP much faster...

"I'm sick and tired of dealing with ghosts!"

But then Asuna jumped up onto the writing desk, nearly kicking the crucial item away as she launched herself into the air. At the top of her jump, she activated the sword skill Shooting Star.

The silver visual effect ran from the tip to the entire weapon—even the body of its wielder—creating an invisible propulsive force. With a twinkling sound effect, Asuna's rapier shot toward the ceiling and caught the ghost square in the chest, gouging a huge hole in its transparent body.

*Ah, I see*, I thought, impressed. *A charging rapier sword skill can hit a pinpoint target with much wider coverage.* The Resentful Wraith issued a hideous, fractal scream and vanished...and the Chivalric Rapier's tip smashed into the ceiling, creating a purple burst of light.

Midair activation of sword skills was a highly technical move that, in essence, allowed you to double jump, but it also had its downsides—if you jumped higher than you intended and suffered fall damage, or if you hit an obstacle and took collision damage. Since we were in town, there was no HP loss for hitting walls or the ceiling, but it struck me as poor form to stand by and watch my partner fall clumsily to the ground.

Therefore, I took two steps forward, estimating where the rebound from hitting the wall of code would send Asuna, and held out my arms. I wasn't entirely confident in my strength stat or my (nonexistent) Carrying skill proficiency, but I did succeed at catching her in a bridal-style hold. When I looked down at her face, I saw hazel-brown eyes blinking back at me.

I thought she was just a bit stunned by the impact, but that didn't seem to be the case. Her mouth opened and closed a few times before she finally squeaked, "Thank you."

"You're welcome."

I set her back on her feet. We both took a deep breath for some reason. It had been an experience, but the haunted house exploration quest was done for now.

"You beat the boss, so you should get the key, Asuna," I urged. The young woman started to approach the writing desk, but she stopped to look down at the bones she'd scattered just moments ago. She turned toward me.

"...Hey, these bones aren't Pithagrus's, are they?"

"Huh? Uh, no...they wouldn't be. Remember, Cylon the disciple killed Pithagrus to become the lord of Stachion and buried his body in the yard behind the mansion."

"Then who do these bones belong to?"

"Um..."

I had to think about this. Because I'd already spoiled the ending, putting the order of the details and story twists together was getting rather complicated.

"...Well, we skipped past that step, but remember how I told you about the proper order of looking up the code to the front-door lock?" I asked.

"Oh, right...you're supposed to go back to Stachion and then look at the painting in the lord's chamber?"

"That's right. And you only know the painting is a hint when Cylon tries to hide it...which would tell you that Cylon knows the digits to that lock are hidden in the painting."

"Oh, I see...But does that really make sense? If he knows the number to unlock this house, why doesn't Cylon come and investigate this place himself? And then he'd find this key. It's the key to whatever place is hiding the golden cube, right?"

I was impressed at the speed of Asuna's understanding and her ability to extrapolate ahead of the information given.

"That's a good point. So the reason he couldn't do that must be because Cylon knows the numbers but not where to use them. Remember? The only person who knew this was Pithagrus's second house was the bartender he would visit—the last person we talked to in Stachion. Pithagrus kept this place a secret from everyone, including his apprentices and servants."

"…But why?"

"You'll know if you check the books in the study."

"Ewww." She grimaced.

In any fantasy RPG, books were a major presence among interior decoration elements. A house should have a bookshelf, and a bookshelf should have books, of course.

But books are one of a game designer's worst enemies. Unlike furniture or utensils, books are made important by their contents. And filling the vast number of in-game books with meaningful content is practically impossible. Therefore, most games either make it impossible to remove the books from the shelf, or they limit access to just a few books, with only a couple pages being viewable.

But *SAO*, likely through some fixation of Akihiko Kayaba's, bravely challenged this limitation. All the books in this world were fully functioning ones that could be taken from the shelf, and all the pages contained print. Generating all that content from scratch was apparently a bridge too far, as nearly all the books simply contained the text of classic books in the public domain as of 2024, in their original languages. So the vast majority of players could look at the books, but reading them was too difficult. I'd heard rumors that some Japanese books were floating around, too, but I'd never seen one.

It was odd to think of books written in real-world languages being on the shelves of a world that contained elves and dwarves and such. But if you started down that road, you'd have to wonder why the NPCs were speaking Japanese, too.

So this was why you could take a book and peruse its contents, but the thought of checking them made even Asuna groan.

"...I feel like I've seen enough Cyrillic and Arabian script to last me a lifetime," she grumbled.

"Don't feel bad. It's all Greek to me...Sorry, sorry, just a joke," I · added when I saw the look she was giving me. "Most of the books in the study are what you'd expect, but a few mixed in are like manuals for puzzles. In other words, Pithagrus the puzzle king kept his secret books with the solutions to the previous lords' puzzles and his own here in his secret home for safekeeping. It's just that if we tried to read them, we wouldn't make any sense of them."

"Ah, I see...Well, I hate to speak ill of the dead, but he sounds like a bit of a miser. Maybe if he'd allowed his apprentices to read these, rather than hogging them all to himself, he wouldn't have wound up getting killed," Asuna said, shaking her head sadly. Then she looked at the bones on the floor. "So...whose bones are these, then?"

"Cylon's henchman. Like us, he heard about the second home from the bar, and he got this far using the combination from Cylon to open the lock...but before he could return to report to his master, the wraiths got him."

"Wait, you mean the person who died here wasn't the wraith we just fought...?"

"If so, then there should have been bones in the other rooms where we found the Annoying Wraiths, right? It seems like once a house is left unattended to fall into ruin, ghosts just naturally swarm there."

"...If I ever buy a player home here, I'm cleaning it every single day. And you're not allowed to leave it cluttered, either, Kirito."

"Yeah, yeah..." I muttered, but then I stopped in my tracks. *Hmm? What sort of a situation is she envisioning in this scenario?* She looked confused by the way I was pondering this, then reflected on what she'd just said, and her white skin instantly turned red.

"No!!"

"O…kay?" I said, startled by her sudden outburst. She grabbed my left shoulder.

"It's not that! It's definitely not that!!"

"O…kay."

I wasn't sure what "that" was, but the point-blank lasers shooting from her eyes convinced me that I should indicate I understood. Asuna snorted, let go of my shoulder, and spun around to head to the desk. She snatched the key and returned in a huff.

"This is the item, right?"

On the left side of my vision, the quest log updated, so I told her, "Yep."

"And what door does this open?"

"Dunno."

"You don't know…?"

"The only person who knows is the one who hid the golden cube and left the key on this desk."

"…So we have to find that person now…" she said, looking briefly crestfallen. But she quickly recovered, opening her game window and putting the key into her inventory. "Yikes, it's after nine already. We'll have to continue tomorrow."

"I agree. Or…I would, but…" I said, considering very carefully how much I ought to spoil. "Well…something's going to happen in a bit that will surprise you, but it definitely won't pose a danger to our lives…In other words, there's no HP loss. So react calmly."

"H-huh? What do you mean…? What's going to happen?"

"Look, I wouldn't want to ruin the best part of a movie for you, would I? Just think of it as a roller coaster and enjoy the ride."

"That does not make me anticipate a good time…" Asuna grumbled, looking around. There was no difference in the walls and shelves surrounding us. Eventually, she summoned her courage, closed her window, then grabbed my shoulders and spun me around.

"You go first, Kirito."

"Got it."

I knew that the order we walked in wasn't going to matter for what happened next, so I stifled my mad grin and started walking back the way we'd come. We passed through the maze of shelves and reached the doorway. Now back in the darkened hallway, I glanced over my shoulder at Asuna's nervous expression, then proceeded toward the distant front door.

On the left, we passed the doors of all the rooms we'd already searched. Soon, the light from the lantern in my left hand reached the entrance hall. It was practically a room of its own, so the light didn't catch every last corner from the hallway. Even knowing that we were safe, and that this was the second time passing through this location, I couldn't help but feel my nerves activating as I stepped into the entryway.

Suddenly, there was a *pshooo!* sound, and a cloud of venomous green smoke ascended to block my vision.

Normally, you'd stand a chance at avoiding a poison mist trap like this if you caught your breath in time, but since this was a forced event, that didn't matter. Behind me, Asuna screamed, and I reached out to grab her hand and keep her calm. The smoke soon reached the level of our faces. The moment I sensed the acrid scent, I felt my legs go numb, and we toppled to the floor.

In the upper left corner, our HP bars were surrounded by borders the color of the smoke. It indicated a paralysis state... but while under normal paralysis you could still use your right arm (barely), now we were completely unable to move—or even speak. Fortunately, the sense of touch was still intact, so through our skin contact, I willed Asuna not to worry.

In thirty seconds, the gas was completely gone without a trace, and the source of it became visible in the light of the lantern, which now lay on the floor. It was a small pot, with a helpful skull symbol on the side. Then there were two sets of approaching footsteps.

In the corner of the entrance hall appeared two men in matching hooded cloaks, large and small—only identifiable as men because I already knew who they were. Beneath their deep hoods, they wore odd leather masks that covered their entire faces.

The large man stopped in the middle of the floor, but the smaller one approached us, then picked up the pot. He put it away in his cloak, then pulled back the hood and removed the mask, which clearly kept him safe from the gas.

"...!!"

I heard Asuna's gasp.

Visible in the orange lantern light were the sunken cheeks, balding head, and impressive beard of the lord of Stachion, Cylon.

"Well, well...I'm quite surprised, swordsman. I did not think you'd find Pithagrus's hideaway so soon. It took me many years to find it...because I never expected it would be in Suribus, rather than Stachion."

He shook his head theatrically, then glanced past me down the hallway. "I am curious about the hidden formula behind his puzzles that he kept so secret...but I'll start with this first."

He walked past me, his oddly upturned shoes clacking against the floor, and reached for Asuna. Through some kind of sleight of hand—or probably just to make the story scene work—the golden key appeared in his palm, when it should have been safe in her inventory. He examined its fine details and exhaled heavily.

"Ahhh...I'd been hoping I would find the cube itself here...but I do have an idea of where I might find the door for this key. Surely, the item I seek will be there," he said, his dejection morphing into a pleasant smile. He tucked the key away into his cloak and stroked his long beard.

"You did very good work for me, swordsman. Normally, this is where I would say farewell...but in fact, I have another job for you to do. Do you mind if I ask for your cooperation once more...?"

He extended his left hand and snapped his fingers. The large masked man, who hadn't said a word, walked over and pulled a large sack from his cloak. He knelt down and grabbed my collar with an abnormally thick fist, easily lifted me up, and tossed me into the sack. I'd experienced this before, but in the beta, I beat the quest on my own. When in a group of two, would they bring out two sacks, or just...?

My question was answered when the mouth of the sack opened again, and my partner landed on top of me. I would've grunted with the impact, if I was able to use my voice yet. Surely, Asuna would not be happy about this, but she'd have to deal with it for the sake of our quest XP.

Over her shoulder, I saw the large man peering into the bag. Then he closed the opening, and we could see nothing.

I could feel the big man hefting us up and over his back. Our sack swayed in rhythm with each plodding footstep. There was the sound of a door opening and closing. Through the heavy burlap, I heard the faint sound of the river and the distant music from NPC musicians.

At this hour, many players would still be eating and shopping in Suribus. And we were being abducted and carried right through all of that—a rather daring setup for a quest. The sack was big enough with the two of us in it; what would happen if it was a full six-man party…? Before I could imagine the possibilities, there was a heavy thump, and we stopped swaying. I could hear sounds of exhaust close by—a horse breathing—and then we were loaded onto a carriage bed.

In moments, the carriage rocked again, probably as the large man and Cylon got into the box seat. There was the sound of a whip cracking, then clopping hooves and rattling wheels. The carriage was slowly making its way down the riverside path.

The paralysis still prevented me from moving or speaking, but knowing that we were getting a free taxi back to Stachion made the experience bearable. The bigger problem was that I had no idea how Asuna—who was resting on top of me—felt about all this. Once we were free to move again, she'd probably scream at me to warn her what was going to happen first, but for now I wanted to believe that she'd understand I was just trying to save the surprise and fun of this climactic scene for her to enjoy.

Within minutes, the carriage was out of town, and the road beneath the wheels turned from paving stone to dirt. It was a mile to Stachion, with no monsters along the way, meaning the trip would be just five minutes long. Naturally, the event would continue after reaching the town, so it would probably be another thirty minutes or so until we fully regained our freedom. At this rate, we'd be spending the night in Stachion, rather than Suribus...

*"Bree-hee-hee!!"*

The carriage came to a violent stop as the horse whinnied. I opened my eyes wide, which was about the only thing I could control, but there was no way to see what was happening outside the sack.

"Who goes there?! I am Cylon, lord of Stachion!" he shouted. It was followed by the sound of metal striking metal.

The horse whinnied again, and the cart tipped over. I would have shouted if I could. The sack tumbled away with us inside it and landed on a short patch of grass. The impact knocked the mouth of the sack slightly open, giving us a better view of the outside.

On top of the carriage, Cylon and a bandit in a black hood were fighting with swords, and a short distance away, the large man in the leather mask was in combat with a similar bandit. Cylon and his assistant's cursors were yellow, while the bandits' were orange.

This event had not happened in the beta. It wasn't that unusual for the quests in the full release to be different, but it did mean that my prior knowledge wasn't going to help anymore. We'd still have to wait for the paralysis to wear off, but once it did, we might be asked to choose between siding with Cylon or the bandits—or just to run away...

"...!!"

I thought I felt Asuna tense and breathe harder than usual.

A moment later, I understood why.

We'd fought a number of forest elves who were treated like NPCs. Their color cursors were red, just like monsters. But the black-hooded bandits fighting Cylon had orange cursors. The color of criminals.

They weren't NPCs. They were *players*.

Just as this dawned on me, the bandit fighting in the bed of the carriage used a sword skill and mercilessly cut down Cylon. The force of the momentum pulled the attacker's hood back, exposing his face.

Glinting in the pale moonlight was a silver chain coif with the ends tattered and hanging—and a large, leering grin underneath.

I knew that face. He had a sword now, but I would never mistake him for anyone else. It was the axman who challenged me to a duel on the third floor with the intent of killing me...

It was Morte.

Cylon's paralyzing poison only immobilized the body and had no effect on the mind of the player—but I couldn't think for several moments.

At last, a question floated into my head—and then the answer. They were as fleeting as bubbles rising and popping.

*What in the world are Morte and his friend doing?*

*...That should be obvious. They're not saving me and Asuna from Cylon. Just the opposite: They're taking advantage of our paralysis to kill us.*

*Then how did they know that we would be paralyzed and passing through this spot at this exact time?*

*...Did they trail us the whole way? No. Morte was a beta tester like me. He would probably know all about the "Curse of Stachion" quest, and he would know that if he staked out Pithagrus's hideout, he would see me and Asuna show up eventually.*

*So how do we escape?*

*.........*

But no amount of waiting brought the answer to the third question to my mind.

It was perfectly possible to interfere with another player's quest if it was happening out in the open, and I'd experienced that in other games before *SAO*. But it never even occurred to me that something like this could have happened.

Cylon was slumped on the floor of the carriage bed, his now-empty sword hand thrust up toward his attacker. "Killing a lord is a grave and terrible crime!" he shouted. "You will never be allowed in Stachion—or through the gates of any other town again!"

I couldn't tell if this line was part of one of Cylon's dialogue patterns or something spontaneous that he came up with when faced with unexpected death. In either case, his threat had no effect on Morte. The axman took two steps forward, still grinning, transferred to a one-handed ax with the Quick Change ability, and brought it down on Cylon's head.

The HP bar underneath the cursor name CYLON went to zero, and the lord of Stachion slowly rocked backward, right hand still outstretched, and tumbled from the cart. His body bounced right near our feet on the ground and came to an unnatural stillness before shattering into a swarm of tiny blue shards.

Like you might expect from a lord, he dropped a number of items among the hoards of gold and silver coins, causing them to jangle and clatter on the ground. It was the kind of profit you'd turn into an orange player to make, but Morte paid it no mind. He gazed down at us from the carriage. His eyes were hidden under the edge of the coif, but the smile on his thin lips grew wider.

Just then, the other hooded bandit fighting the larger man on the other side of the carriage screeched, "Hey, if you're done with the old man, help me out! This fat-ass is pretty high-level!"

I craned my eyes as far as they could go and saw the large man, his huge fists wrapped in leather straps studded with metal, swinging at the smaller hooded player nimbly darting around. The bandit had a thin dagger in his hand, which told me he must be the one who was meeting with Morte in the underground catacombs on the fifth floor. If these two were around, then it was possible that the boss of the PK gang was nearby—the man in the black poncho who tried to kill me during the fireworks show—but I didn't sense him yet.

The dagger user darted around the large man's punches and struck back deftly, but he maintained his distance and wasn't getting close enough to do big damage. At this point, our only hope was to rely on the man who had stuck us in this sack in the first place. If he could hold out for a few minutes, even with Morte involved, Asuna and I might recover from our paralysis.

But...

"Sorry, I'm busy right now. If you can't take him out, then pull him into the forest and lose him there, please," Morte commanded, then turned back to us. His partner protested, but it seemed clear that Morte held a higher position in their gang. Instead, he yelled at the large man to follow him and raced into the thick woods on the south side of the road. The man in the leather mask issued a muffled roar and pounded after him.

When the two pairs of footsteps had vanished, there was a deafening silence left behind. For some reason, the usual calls of the night insects and owls hooting were completely gone.

Into that silence landed the sound of light feet. Morte had jumped from the bed of the carriage. The ax he'd used to kill Cylon rested on his shoulder, and he stepped carelessly over the scattered coins on the ground as he approached me and Asuna where we lay.

"...Well, well, well. I've been awaiting you, Kirito. I had a feeling you'd accept the lord's quest, but I wasn't so positive that I was gonna follow you the whole way from the start. Instead, I just sat watching Py-whatsit's hideout from an inn starting last night...Oh! Whoopsie."

His leer turned a bit embarrassed, and he scratched the side of his head with the back of the ax.

"Boss always tells me I oughta watch out about talkin' too much, but it doesn't look like that's ever going to change, does it? On the other hand, it'd really suck if you recovered from your paralysis while I'm just chatting on and on, so I'm afraid this is where we say good-bye."

He spun the ax in his fingers, twirling it audibly, then gripped it straight and began to walk again.

Just at that moment, the green border around my and Asuna's HP bars began to blink. Thirty seconds until the debuff wore off naturally…but five seconds was all he'd need to kill a defenseless player.

Asuna was sprawled on her side with her back to me, so I couldn't see her face. I couldn't say a word to her or hold her hand.

I let this situation come about due to my own lack of caution. I knew we'd be carried out of town in a totally helpless state, and I should have realized that this would leave us vulnerable to possible PKers. And even if I hadn't figured it out, perhaps Asuna would have been observant enough to spot my folly, if I hadn't been so preoccupied with my precious story surprises.

I had to find a way to get Asuna out of this death trap, even if it required sacrificing myself.

The boots crunched closer.

The debuff wasn't gone yet.

My heart jackhammered.

This wasn't a virtual signal. I knew that wherever I was in the real world, my heart was racing there, too. My mind was compressed, time passing slower than it should, as my brain sped through all possible choices.

I could see Asuna's chestnut-brown hair, the green grass, and the navy forest in the background…as well as the assortment of items Cylon dropped upon his death. Gold coins, silver, mysterious pouches, a rather expensive-looking longsword, his leather mask, an iron key, a golden key, a small jar, and those shoes with the upturned toes.

A possibility shot through my mind, as instantaneous as lightning.

I couldn't move my arms or legs at the moment. But there were two things I *could* do.

One was look. The other was breathe.

Morte came to a stop just a foot and a half behind me; I was lying on my side. While I couldn't see him directly, his shadow was black on the ground, silently raising the ax high over his head.

At that moment, I expelled the lungful of air I was holding through pursed lips.

I was aiming for the small jar, which was standing upright about three feet away. It had a skull mark on the side—it was what Cylon had used to paralyze us. It must have reinitialized in its default state when it dropped, because it was stopped up closed rather than open and empty.

The jar was only two inches tall, and exhaled breath here tended to be exaggerated—we'd been able to blow up the inner-tube fruits on the fourth floor with a single breath—but I wasn't sure if I'd be able to knock it over. To my surprise, however, another gust of air descended upon it at the same time. Asuna had come to the same conclusion and attempted the same trick.

The little jar lurched sideways with the force of two breaths at once. It tilted back, lurched forward—and toppled. The lid, which was simply resting in place, rolled off onto the ground, and that vicious green smoke shot out with startling force. I sucked in a huge, deep breath of clean air and held it.

Instantly, the smoke enveloped us, turning everything green. I heard the clicking of a tongue and sensed Morte scurrying away. The blinking of the green border around my HP gauge grew quicker and quicker.

In Aincrad, raising two different kinds of stats could allow you to exhibit physical strength and speed that were impossible in real life. But there *were* a few scant things in a full-dive VRMMO that were still derived from your actual physical body.

One of those things was lung capacity. If water covered your head, the game registered you in the Drowning state, but as long as you held your breath, there would be no HP loss. Since that breath was not only the avatar's, but your physical body's, that meant that players who had higher lung capacity in the real world could move around longer underwater. The same property applied to holding your breath against poison gas.

I didn't get much exercise in elementary or middle school, so my confidence in my lung capacity was low, but Cylon's gas had only lasted for thirty seconds at the haunted house, and I knew I could at least hold it that long. The problem was whether the paralysis still had that much time left...and if Morte would stay clear for the full thirty seconds.

It had been five...six...seven seconds since the gas started—and the HP bar border and debuff icon were gone. Instantly, feeling returned to my body, and I pushed myself up with my left hand, reaching for my sword with my right.

That was when Morte came charging through the curtain of poison toward me.

The gas was so thick that I could only see a vague outline of the enemy's shape. The same was true for Morte, but the blow he hurled, cutting through the smoke, was perfectly aimed at my face.

If I blocked the head of the ax swooping toward me with my sword alone, I would lose in terms of weight and momentum. But I also didn't have time to slash at it from a crouched position. I had no choice but to put my left hand up behind the blade and assume a two-handed blocking pose.

Morte's ax smashed against the side of the Sword of Eventide, spraying sparks that were nearly blinding, even in the thick haze. The impact was so strong that I was briefly afraid my sword would break, but the Yofilis clan's legendary blade absorbed it valiantly—the rebound buckling Morte's stance slightly.

"......!!"

I bolted up with a dull roar, executing the basic martial arts skill Flash Blow with my left hand. My fist shot forward wreathed in red light, which Morte blocked with his clenched right arm—but not solidly enough to keep himself from tipping off-balance. I had a post-skill pause, too, but of all the sword skills I knew, Flash Blow had the shortest delay. When I recovered less than a second later, Morte was still reeling.

His right side was guarded by his tough-looking ax, but his left was defenseless. The best way to strike him there would be with the longsword skill Horizontal—

No. Wait.

When I fought Morte at the forest elf camp on the third floor, he used Quick Change to switch his sword for his ax. But he also brought up a round shield alongside the ax. But now his left hand was empty. Did he change his style? Why—?

To make me think his left hand was empty.

"‼"

I gritted my teeth and stopped myself from using the sword skill I was just about to cue up, pulling back my blade. At the same moment, Morte snapped his left wrist and threw something at my face.

The object split the poison gas and deflected off my sword, which I barely lifted in time. Based on the loud metallic *clang* and the strength of impact, I could guess that it was a throwing pick—probably poisoned.

In the time that I drew my sword back to defend, Morte had recovered, but he chose to withdraw rather than counterattack. He jumped backward, and I followed, careful for any additional throwing darts. In five seconds, I was out of the poison gas, so I expelled my breath and sucked in fresh air.

Five yards up ahead, Morte took a breath of his own, his mouth wide with glee.

"Ha-ha…Well done, Kirito. I can't believe you blocked that."

"Say, wherever did you get that very dangerous and rare poisoned pick?" I asked him, glancing at the polished Sword of Eventide to see what was reflected in its surface from behind me. Asuna recovered at the same time I did, but she hadn't left the green smoke yet. The debuff icon was gone from her HP bar, so

I knew she hadn't sucked in a new dose of it, but I didn't know what reason she might have for not moving yet.

"Well, if I told you that, you'd go and get it yourself, wouldn't you? It's surprising how useful these things can be," Morte leered, reaching down to draw a fresh one from his belt.

Poison in *SAO*—especially the paralyzing kind—was incredibly dangerous, as evidenced by the way he'd nearly used that paralysis event to kill us. For that reason, it was very, very hard for players to make use of it. Not only was it difficult enough to craft a high-level paralysis agent with the Mixing skill, spreading it on your weapon alone did not have any effect. The weapon itself needed to have an extremely rare Toxicity attribute, and I'd never even seen a weapon like that, much less found one. The man in the black poncho, Morte's boss, had claimed the knife he had on my back was augmented with level-5 paralysis and level-5 poison, but I later discovered that was just a bluff.

But the four-inch pick Morte had between his fingers was shining with oily residue under the light of the moon. He'd clearly given up on his shield and accepted the "irregular equipment" status that made him ineligible to use sword skills, all just so he could perform sneak attacks with this thing, so it had to be a poisoned weapon. Whatever solution he'd put on it, I was not going to let him hit me.

Fortunately, picks were disposable weapons by nature, with both buyable and droppable versions coming in sets of three. The first one Morte threw went into the forest somewhere, so he had two left. If I could remove them from the equation, I had the advantage.

Morte's leer softened a bit. He pushed his ax forward and hid his throwing hand behind it. I set my sword up at mid-level, ready to deflect from any angle.

The poison gas behind me was still there. It only lasted thirty seconds when Cylon had gassed us, so I assumed it would be the same here—but what if the activation period was compressed just for the event, and once it had dropped for a player, its default length was longer? If it was two minutes, or even just one, I couldn't guarantee that Asuna's breath would hold out. If the paralysis was gone, why wasn't she emerging from the smoke...?

Right as I started to get legitimately worried, I heard a screech from the far side of the smoke cloud.

"Whew! Finally lost him! Hey, you all done over there yet?"

The second hooded man who'd pulled the NPC into the woods returned sooner than I expected. I gnashed my teeth, while Morte's smile returned. If Asuna was in some kind of trouble and couldn't get free, I'd have to fight one-on-two while protecting her. In fact, her life was the top priority, so if need be, I'd have to sacrifice myself so that my partner could escape.

In the flat of my blade, my impromptu rearview mirror, I saw a dark hooded figure skirt the poison cloud at a wide distance.

"...Damn, he's still alive? What's up with this smoke anyway? We weren't supposed to be usin' this, right?"

"It's not mine. Kirito here found a way to utilize the NPC's poison item. Aha-ha-ha," Morte replied.

The second hood clicked his tongue theatrically. "What a pain in the ass. On the other hand...maybe I'm lucky, now that I get to finish someone off? I still haven't gotten over my rage at having my Cilvaric Rapier stolen from me on the fifth floor. Hey, where's the woman?"

"She still seems to be paralyzed inside the smoke cloud."

"Cool. Then let's kill the beater over there first."

Hood Number Two pulled a dark, gleaming dagger from his waist.

I maintained my silence while the other two talked on either side of me, but the instant Number Two mentioned Asuna, I felt my blood boil and nearly leaped to the attack. But I knew that the instant I turned my back to Morte, he'd throw the pick. The Coat of Midnight I'd powered up at the dark elf camp was still powerful enough to hang here on the sixth floor, despite it being the Last Attack bonus prize for beating the boss on the very first floor. The problem was that it was weak to piercing attacks, like all nonmetal armor. It was only a minor deal in Aincrad, where there were no bows and arrows, but alongside polearms like spears and lances—and one-handed weapons like estocs and stilettos—throwing picks were a perfectly serviceable kind of piercing weapon.

I'd rush Morte as fast as I could to neutralize them, then defeat his comrade. That was the only way out of this—but could I actually overpower the axman, knowing that his dueling ability was probably sharper since the last time we fought? Even if I had the technique and statistics, could I *myself* cross that final line...?

Unlike in the real world, as long as you had a single pixel of health left on your gauge, you could move and fight. So the only way to guarantee his neutralization without poison or traps was to reduce his HP to zero—to kill him.

Because Morte and the dagger user had attacked Cylon and his assistant, their player cursors were orange, the color of criminals. As a green player, I could attack them without penalty or fear of turning orange myself, but that was only going by the rules of the system. At the present moment, *SAO* was an inescapable death game, and losing your HP meant the NerveGear would fry your brain with intense microwaves. If I killed Morte and his friend, I would be killing their biological bodies, wherever they were in the real world.

Player-killing was actual murder now. Could I do that?

Demonic intuition saw right through me in that moment of indecision.

*"Shah!"*

Morte hissed into movement. I jumped to my left to get out of the way and to keep the dagger user in sight. But Morte read that all the way and turned the same direction with me, swiping sideways with his ax.

As long as he was holding the poison needle in his left hand, he'd be registered as dual-wielding—and unable to use sword skills. But Morte's one-handed ax had a power that couldn't be overlooked, even using just ordinary attacks. Unlike the Anneal

Blade and its excellent weight and toughness, the Sword of Eventide was sharp but light, and it might not stand up to tough attacks if my guarding technique wasn't thorough.

When I landed, I swayed backward, and the thick blade of the ax roared directly where my neck had been. The swing was so heavy that Morte ended up exposing his back to me. Despite my stance, I could've attacked him from that position, but Hood Number Two was bearing down on me with his dagger. If they trapped me front and back in the open, I'd get hit by that poison pick eventually. I needed to lure them to the woods on the north side of the road so that I could fight with my back against a tree.

I bent my knees, ready to jump again.

Just then, the green cloud of smoke behind Number Two split down the middle.

It was a fencer, dark red hooded cape flapping behind her, silver rapier in her hand. Her face was hidden behind a monstrous leather mask—the gas mask Cylon used in Pithagrus's hideaway and dropped upon his death. Asuna had been lurking in the midst of the gas for over a minute because she'd been wearing it.

Both Morte, who was trying to pull his ax momentum back toward me, and the onrushing Hood Number Two, failed to notice her. She could take the advantage by using a sword skill against the second one's defenseless back.

But the question was: Could Asuna, who'd never experienced a duel as a form of truly mortal combat, actually do this? If she hesitated for even an instant during activation, the skill would fumble, and she'd be frozen in place, open to a devastating counter.

All through this moment of breath-stopping apprehension, I kept my focus on Morte's ax. If my expression caused Number Two to realize the back attack, Asuna's patience and trickery would be lost. I had to believe in my partner.

*"Shhu!"*

Morte swung the ax again. I stepped backward only as little as I needed to avoid it, keeping my eyes on his left hand. He was looking for me to block the ax, giving him an opening to throw his pick, so I had to keep out of the way with swaying and quickstepping.

Out of the corner of my eye, I saw Asuna racing at incredible speed to close the gap, pulling back her rapier to strike. Her target was rapidly slowing, perhaps noticing the footsteps behind him. The fierce point of her weapon shone a brilliant red. Asuna's right arm and sword melted into the flow of light. As I prepared for Morte's third strike, I sent a silent message to my partner.

*Go, Asuna!!*

There was a series of heavy impacts. Her sword skill Triangular hit the man right in the back, knocking off over a third of his health.

"Aaah...crap!" he grunted in pain and fury, doing a roll and a half over the ground with his back bleeding a huge damage visual effect, but he did bounce up onto his feet rather than enter a fallen state.

"She ain't paralyzed! That was a dirty trick!" he yelled.

Asuna recovered from her post-skill delay and, ignoring his hypocritical protest, pulled off her leather mask and tossed it to the grass. In the pale moonlight, her beautiful features were fierce with an anger—the likes of which I'd never seen. It was enough to shut up the screeching man, that was for sure.

"Leave this one to me. You get Morte, Kirito."

Her quiet voice arrived loud and clear at a distance of over thirty feet. I gave her cold, glowing eyes the briefest of nods, then turned to the axman.

The cruel mouth visible beneath his coif did not contain the slightest hint of a smile any longer. "Oh, my," he growled. "Our fun has turned into a real predicament, very quickly."

"You thought you were going to have an easy time killing some immobilized people? Think again."

"Now, now, it's not settled yet. I still have two poison...picks!" he shouted, flipping the ax in his right hand up vertically. I leaned back on instinct as the darkened blade rushed toward my nose.

It hurt not to be able to guard, but Morte's Harsh Hatchet was upgraded with +6 to Heaviness, which was enough to weigh down the avatar's center of gravity at the start of the swing. It was a very minor tell, but if you were watching for it, you could notice.

While Morte and I were locked in combat, Asuna and Hood Number Two were going at it with quite spectacular results.

Both were speed types—the dagger and rapier flashing with dizzying speed, lighting up the night with a shower of sparks. In terms of pure speed, none of the frontline players could surpass Asuna—if anyone could do it, Argo's extreme AGI build might do the trick. But in a player-on-player fight with no rules, her style was just a little too straightforward. Against an opponent well versed in feints and tricks, she was likely to meet stiff competition.

But after she'd fallen onto her seat in simple practice bouts against me, the fact that she was putting her all into a fight against a true PKer was a sign of huge progress. I had to match her example. I couldn't stay on the defensive this whole time.

Morte continued swinging furiously at me, trying to force me to block his ax—or just knock me off-balance so he could stab me with the needle directly. In the real world, he would be out of breath by now, but as long as you didn't perform actions beyond your strength variable, the hidden "fatigue quotient" would not be a problem here.

The forest at night offered poor visibility and uneven footing, so if I kept dodging, I was bound to trip over a root or stone eventually. I had to break out of this situation before that happened.

"Sh…shwaa!"

I evaded Morte's consecutive swipes, sideways then vertical, with quick, narrow footwork. Then I gambled: I pretended to trip on something, slumping forward.

Morte pounced. "Haaaa!" he hissed, swinging the Harsh Hatchet from above. He was stepping in quite far, since I'd been pulling back with all of my evasion.

Axes were powerful whether equipped in one hand or two,

but if you got close enough—and you used all your boldness and bravery—you could take advantage of their structural weakness.

"Argh!" I shouted, tensing my bent, "tripping" left leg and launching myself forward off it. That pushed me inside of the falling ax head's path, where I could reach up with my left forearm and brace it against the ax handle.

A fierce shock ran through my arm and shoulder, and I lost about 5 percent of my HP. But at the same time, I activated the sword skill Slant with my other hand. The glowing blue blade struck Morte's left arm as he was pulling his wrist back to flick the poisoned projectile.

I figured that if I could get him to drop the pick, great. But my dark elf masterpiece showed even greater ability in answering my risky gamble. The sword silently sliced Morte's arm off below the elbow. His forearm burst into tiny crystal pieces, and the pick he was holding fell to the grass.

I'd caused part-loss damage. He couldn't throw his picks with his left hand for at least three minutes, when he would recover from this effect.

"Ha-ha!" Morte chuckled, either as a bluff or a sign that he still had tricks up his sleeve. He jumped backward, vivid red particles spilling from his severed arm like blood.

I wasn't the type to pursue further attacks in a duel after I'd already struck home. Throwing together sword skills in pursuit of maximum damage also maximized your own vulnerability, and it was very easy to suffer devastating consequences when caught up in the moment.

But in this one instance, as soon as my skill delay was over, I rushed forward, chasing after Morte as he withdrew. It seemed I was angrier than I realized at the PKers for going after Asuna… and at myself, for not recognizing the danger of the paralysis event.

"Raaahh!!" I bellowed from deep in my gut, thrusting the sword with a twist of my wrists. Multiple traces of pale blue light shot from its tip, and an invisible force pushed me from behind. It was the low thrusting skill, Rage Spike.

This sword skill, which unlocked at a one-handed sword's proficiency of 50, was one of the basic skills after Slant, Vertical, and Horizontal. So it had low power, but unlike Sonic Leap, which involved jumping high and striking downward, it thrust in a straight line along the ground, making it more accurate and harder to defend against.

With his left hand gone and no longer wielding weapons in both hands, Morte was now free to use sword skills with his ax, but seeing me bent over and racing along the ground, he instantly abandoned the idea of countering. He flipped the ax over and held it before him to guard.

The ax's handle was essentially just a round stick, though some could have spikes or little blades of their own. But because of that structure, it was the weapon's weak point during attack—though unlike swords, an ax's shaft was much less likely to be destroyed when defending, no matter how it was struck. And with Morte's skill, he wouldn't have too much trouble guarding my thrust with the handle, even one less than an inch thick.

However, a thrust when blocked could still knock back the target. Now was the time to put everything into this strike without fear of reprisal—to let him know what he was dealing with.

"Yaaa!" I bellowed, unleashing my sword straight for his chest.

"Sshheh!" Morte hissed, brandishing the ax handle in the path of the pale blue line. The tip of my sword rushed forward, ready to split that steel pole.

And then.

As though the sword moved on its own, the tip swayed just a tiny bit to the right. The perfectly hard, implacable Sword of Eventide, in this single moment, took on a living suppleness, twisting itself to evade its obstacle…or so it seemed to me.

It grazed the edge of the Harsh Hatchet just enough to create sparks, then regained its usual hardness, striking an inch to the right of Morte's center—directly into his heart, a critical point—with terrifying accuracy.

The axman's slim-fitting, dark gray scale armor was wetly

semi-reflective, suggesting that it was made not of metal, but some monster-hide material. It looked easy to move in and quiet, ideal for PKing, but its ability to deflect piercing and thrusting attacks was no different from my long coat's.

So the Sword of Eventide, rather than stopping as it would against some thick metal plate, sliced through the gaps between scales and sank deeper and deeper...

*Kadaaamm!!* I'd used this skill more times than I could count, and even I'd never heard it produce that kind of blast. It vibrated through my palm hard enough to shake my very skull. The lighting effect the impact produced was two or three times brighter than usual, making my vision go hazy and blue.

Sound, light, feedback. This was a true critical hit. *And* a weak-point crit, too.

When the flash subsided, over half my sword was embedded in Morte's chest.

The HP bar in the middle of the orange cursor floating over the axman's head began to dwindle. It seemed to move slower than usual, perhaps because I was in a state of heightened alert, but it showed no signs of stopping. From a nearly full position, it dropped to 70, then 60, then 50 percent and lower, into the yellow warning zone.

I was certain it would stop soon, but the yellow line continued narrowing at the same steady pace. It was down to 40 percent, then 35...and 30. Now into the red warning zone, the bar headed ever closer to the left end of the gauge.

When he'd challenged me to the half-finish duel on the third floor, Morte softened me down to just over half my HP so he could destroy the remainder in one final blow—a duel PK. But ultimately, that fight ended with both HP bars at just over 50 percent.

25...23...it kept going. Was it possible to completely eradicate all of a high-level player's HP in a single blow, even with a true crit against a weak point? Glowing red light spilled from where the elven sword stuck into Morte's chest, pulsing like blood. Through the palm of my right hand, I felt a trembling like a heartbeat. Neither I nor Morte budged an inch.

A number of times in the past, I'd suffered so much damage at once that I couldn't even breathe, much less move, while my HP bar dropped. That was hard enough in the beta, but now the consequences of death were permanent. If it didn't stop, then Morte…the guy lying on some bed somewhere in Japan…would be put to death by his NerveGear.

Without realizing it, I glanced from his red HP bar to the face under his chain coif. The red light pouring from his heart cast a faint glow on the upper half of his face, which was consistently sunken in shadow otherwise.

My first glance at the PKer showed me an ordinary young man, maybe a few years older than me but still a teenager. His gaping eyes stared at the space over my right shoulder…at the HP bar of mine that only he could see. He wore no true expression, but his lips, which were normally curled into a sneer, now parted slightly, as if mouthing disbelief.

My mouth was open, too, and I wanted to ask him, even if just through the movement of my lips, why he would ever choose to PK in a world like this one…

…when a voice in an extremely grating, high-pitched register pierced my eardrums from behind.

"Mamoru! Pull the sword ouuuut!!"

In an instant, I finally understood.

Morte's HP hadn't dropped this far just from the combined critical hit. He was suffering continuous piercing damage. With my sword still stuck in him, his HP continued to bleed out of him.

When he realized this, too, Morte let out an uncharacteristic, panicked wail. He dropped the Harsh Hatchet and grabbed the Sword of Eventide's blade with his right hand.

If I clutched the handle of the sword with both hands and pushed it toward the hilt, I could kill him in less than five seconds.

And I probably ought to. He tried to use the paralysis event to kill Asuna and me. If he survived this, he would probably try something similar again. I didn't want to die, and I especially didn't want Asuna to die. She was going to grow into a far greater warrior than me, lead the game's population to victory, and save thousands of lives.

Nothing was more important than Asuna's life.

So it was utterly crucial that I took this step now, to——

"Aaaah! *Aaaaaaah!!*"

There was a scream behind me—a sound not even human. Footsteps rushed toward me.

On instinct, I put my left hand on Morte's chest and pulled the Sword of Eventide free. Red particles scattered from the blade as I swung it, right as Black Hood Number Two leaped at me with his dagger drawn.

Asuna was in pursuit behind him, but the man's foot speed was formidable, and she wouldn't reach him in time. I stepped to the right and held up my sword, preparing to meet the dagger even as I kept an eye on Morte, in case he decided to throw his third pick with his one good hand.

But Morte stayed down and immobile, and Black Hood Number Two engaged in some unexpected strategy. He hurled his dagger at me without so much as pausing to aim it.

A single swing of my sword knocked the spinning dagger aside. Then Number Two threw something with his other hand.

It wasn't a weapon, but a small sphere slightly over an inch in size. I'd just seen the same object less than thirty hours earlier, so I ran toward Asuna and shouted, "Stop! It's a smoke bomb!"

There was a soft, deep *boomf!* behind me. I turned back as I reached her and saw a curtain of smoke darker than night rising to cover the PKers.

Even still, I could see the dagger man grabbing Morte's right hand and helping him up. Then thick smoke covered their silhouettes, and I heard only faint footsteps racing toward the forest to the north and out of earshot. The two orange cursors blinked out at the same time.

I already knew the smoke screen didn't confer any system

debuffs. So if I chased after them, there was a high possibility I could take them both out for good—or at least the gravely wounded Morte.

But my feet felt so heavy that my knees sank into the grass, and Asuna made no move after them, either.

The cold night breeze swished through the trees, finally dispersing the green poison gas and the fresh, dark smoke screen. When the air had cleared, Asuna dropped her Chivalric Rapier into the sheath at her side and muttered, "What did he mean, 'Mamoru'? If he hadn't said that, I wouldn't have hesitated about chasing them."

While Morte had been suffering that continuous damage, Black Hood Number Two had called him Mamoru. It was either a nickname between comrades, or…I had to stop myself from continuing that thought—and put my sword back where I normally kept it.

"I was almost there, but I wasn't able to go through with killing him. When I drew my sword, I was so certain I would never let him do the same thing again…"

"…I wonder if they'll come back," Asuna murmured.

I thought it over for a bit. "They probably will. And they'll have some new kind of PK scheme that we could never see coming…"

After I said that, I realized there was something else I should've said right away. I turned to Asuna, looked into her curious eyes for a third of a second, then looked away and bowed my head to her.

"I'm sorry, Asuna. I knew the abduction event was going to take us out of town in a paralyzed state, so I should've realized this could happen…and because I wasn't thinking straight, I exposed you to danger. I'm really, truly sorry."

Upon further reflection, I'd earned Asuna's anger on numerous occasions since our partnership began on the first floor. I couldn't even recall the exact number of times she'd thrown a pillow or jabbed me in the side on this floor alone.

But this mistake was on a different level. If I hadn't given her my careless guarantee, backed by beta experience, that it was "absolutely safe"—or if I'd just told her exactly what would happen in the event—Asuna's perspective without prior influence might have noticed the danger of PKing it harbored.

The peril we just survived was clearly a situation that came about because I was a beater. And I couldn't guarantee that it would be the last time.

"…I feel like I probably don't have the right to continue being your par…" I started to say until something soft brushed the sides of my lowered head.

I realized they were Asuna's hands. She pulled me upward, forcing me to stand straight. The young woman glared right at my face, not removing her grip.

"I'm going to tell you one thing I really, truly hate."

"Y…yes?"

"It's when two people know what each other are thinking, but they decide to continue using vague, imprecise words to keep everything at a distance and play oblique mind games. Yes, softening things is valuable sometimes, but the really important things ought to be said cleanly and clearly…don't you agree?"

"Um…Wh-what are we talking about…?"

I understood the point Asuna was making, I just didn't know how it connected to the present situation. But with her holding my head tight in both hands, I couldn't even put a finger to my cheek to ponder this.

"My question is," Asuna said, sucking in a deep breath, "are you saying you want to break up our partnership?"

With no escape from this direct fastball of a question, I had little choice but to answer honestly. "If it's a matter of wanting to or not wanting to…I don't want us to split up."

"Okay. Well, neither do I…so that should be our conclusion. Right?"

"………"

*She is such a stud*, I thought bizarrely. Asuna ruffled her hands wildly over my head before letting go.

"Now that that's settled, there are plenty of things we need to talk over...What do you think we should do first?"

"Um...ummmmm..."

I sucked in a lungful of the cold, refreshing, midwinter air that shrouded the forest to reset my mind and glanced around us.

We'd moved farther than I thought during the battle. The packed dirt path was about twenty-five feet to the south of us. The riderless carriage and horse were still on the road. It seemed like we should do something about that, but I had no idea what. Plenty of glittering objects littered the ground around the carriage, too. Thousand-col gold coins, hundred-col silvers, and a wide variety of items. All had belonged to Lord Cylon of Stachion before Morte killed him.

"...How about we figure out what to do later but grab the stuff Cylon dropped fir..." I started to say, before I realized something.

There was one item we needed to grab right away. I tore my gaze away from the carriage and back to the grass. "Asuna, find the ax and dagger they dropped!" I shouted.

Then I ran a few yards and leaned into the thick undergrowth. It was around here, I was certain. I needed the spot where I'd cut off Morte's left arm; he'd had the poisoned pick in that hand when it happened. And the moment his severed hand vanished, the pick had...

"...Aha!"

I reached into the grass and carefully hefted a black piece of metal stuck into the ground. It was a little less than four inches long—and three-tenths of an inch at the thickest point—with six sides that curved gently, prompting me to think of a type of drill bit. From the middle to the needle-like point at the end, an oily liquid seemed to be oozing from the inside of the spiral grooves.

I was curious to check its item properties, but the ownership and equipment status of this pick were still with Morte, and I had to do whatever it took to steal it from him. If they got to a safe location and used the Materialize All Items command, the pick would instantly vanish. And in fact, Morte might not even need to bother with such a thing.

"I got them, Kirito," said Asuna, trotting over with an ax in her right hand and a dagger in her left. I consulted my mental list of the various monsters one could encounter in the fields of the sixth floor.

I knew there was one. One of those detestable creatures with the same habits as the ratmen lurking in the catacombs of the fifth floor. It was called...

"...Asuna, go and look in the surrounding forest to see if there's a monster called a Muriqui Snatcher."

"Moo-reekee...? That's a weird name. How do you spell it?"

"Uh, it's tricky...M-u-r-i-q-u-i, I think."

"Hmm..."

Even Asuna, whose knowledge sometimes seemed encyclopedic, didn't recognize that word. It occurred to me that I should've looked it up in the two months between the end of the beta test and the launch of the game. I scanned the woods on the north side of the path but didn't see any shapes that looked like the monster in question.

Monsters weren't designed to populate the areas right around roads, even in the danger of the wilderness, but that only applied when players were quiet and minding their own business. I'd been worried that the screeching of the dagger user trying to save Morte might have brought the monsters down upon us, but fortunately—or in this case, unfortunately—there hadn't been any in range of his shouting.

That meant we'd have to go into the forest to find one, but would it be in time? Morte and his group were already criminals, so they couldn't go into any town or village, making it difficult to find a safe harbor—but they would've been aware of that when devising this plan. If they had an evacuation area somewhere nearby, it would come down to whether they reached it first—or we found a Muriqui Snatcher...

"—rito. Hey, Kirito."

The mention of my name caused me to snap to attention. My partner was pointing not to the north, but behind me to the south. I turned and looked to the darkened woods.

*"Ooh...oo-ooh!"*

The sound of calls vaguely humanoid and animalistic came into hearing range, and I noticed a number of small silhouettes among the tree branches. Above their heads, reddish cursors that identified them as monsters sprang into being. There were ten—no more than fifteen of them.

"Look! They're all muriquis!" Asuna pointed out. Indeed, all of their displayed names began with Muriqui, but this was no situation for celebration.

I was level 19 at the moment, and Asuna was at 18. This was considerably higher than the needed level at the start of the sixth floor, so all the cursors were only a pale pink color, but they were numerous. And there weren't just the Snatchers that I wanted, but others like Muriqui Brawlers and Muriqui Nut Throwers were in the mix as well. It turned out the man's screech was quite effective after all; he'd called down an entire pack of muriquis that normally stayed deep in the woods.

All players in *SAO* were capable of producing the same vocal volume, but because it sampled the actual voice of the player for use in the environment, the tenor of your voice made a difference in how well it carried. The dagger user had a hideous, shrieking voice that refused to blend into the natural ambience and was bound to carry farther, even in the noisy night forest. Being able to gather a wide range of monsters just by screaming was an effective ability for a PKer—not that I thought that was why he chose to engage in the activity.

"So...what now?" Asuna asked.

It was directed at me, of course, but a number of the muriquis descended from the tree branches down vines and trunks as though answering that query. *Hoo-hoo*, they called, approaching the abandoned carriage. Once out from under the tree canopy, the moonlight illuminated their forms.

"Oh…they're monkeys," Asuna remarked. Indeed, the muriquis were monkey-type monsters with furry coats, tails, and long arms. They were much smaller than the apes that appeared in higher floors and only four feet tall when upright, but they were also very quick, and they made use of the trees to leap about in three dimensions in aggravating ways.

Four of them had gone to the ground—three of which were Snatchers with kangaroo-like pouches on their bellies, and the last was a Brawler with a club-like stick in its hand. Asuna and I could eliminate these four in an instant with sword skills, but attacking would probably bring the other dozen down on us from the trees. We'd been training and completing quests non-stop since this morning, and just after this fight to the death against Morte and his friend, I was sure that Asuna was more exhausted than she let on. In order to permanently seize the mysterious poisoned needle and their melee weapons, battle against the muriquis would be unavoidable. The only question was how hard to push ourselves.

As I mulled this quandary over, the trio of Snatchers approached the rear of the carriage and began picking up the coins and stuffing them into their stomach pouches. Asuna seemed a bit perturbed by this.

"H-hey, they're picking up Cylon's things!"

"Yeah, that's the idea," I muttered. She glared at me skeptically.

Just then, the heavy ax dangling from her grip vanished with a *shwim!* sound effect.

*We were too late*, I lamented—but then I realized that the dagger and poisoned pick in my hands were still there. That meant the two PKers hadn't gotten to an evacuation point and used Materialize All Items; Morte had just used Quick Change to retrieve his main weapon, the one-handed ax.

Since the same thing hadn't happened to these items, that meant the dagger user didn't have the Quick Change mod yet.

Still, the all-crucial poisoned pick was likely to vanish within the next minute. All Morte had to do was switch the item registered to the Quick Change icon from the ax to the pick, then use the skill again.

Better to let a monster pick it up than just have it taken away, so I hurled it at the feet of the Muriqui Snatchers. I commanded my partner, "Throw the dagger in the same spot!"

"O-okay."

Asuna tossed the black dagger. One of the Snatchers approached, hooting, and quickly scooped both the pick and dagger into its pouch. They had the Robbing skill, so ownership of the items instantly transferred, and neither Quick Change nor Materialize All Items could remotely recover them. Once the pack of muriquis finished taking all the items, they'd retreat deep into the forest, so the odds were nearly zero that Morte and his friend would find the right monkeys to defeat them and take their weapons back.

I told myself that this course of action was for the best...and turned to Asuna so that I could suggest we head back to town. But before I could, she murmured, "I see. I finally understand... You wanted to do the same method as when you got my rapier back on the fifth floor."

"Wha—?"

"Let's beat them before they get away! You get the one with the stick, Kirito!"

*She is such a bundle of energy*, I couldn't help but marvel, before I snapped out of it and hurried after my partner.

Once it was all over, I realized the pack of sixteen muriquis hadn't been as dangerous as I'd feared.

Because we fought them near the road rather than in the woods, they couldn't use their nimble simian evasion techniques through the trees. The worst part ended up being the Muriqui Nut Throwers tossing hard shells at us from behind, but once you got used to them, it was pretty easy to swat the projectiles out of the air. Also, the Snatchers usually ran as soon as you attacked them when alone, but in a pack, they would stand their ground to the end. This made it quite easy to ensure we got back all the items the trio of Snatchers took.

If anything, the biggest problem for us was *after* the battle with the monkeys, when Cylon's large assistant plodded back out of the trees. I'd completely forgotten about him, but now that the second attacker had left him behind in the woods, he'd faithfully returned to his carriage.

I was worried it would turn into another fight, but the man in the gas mask simply plodded up to the box of the horse cart and drove it down the road to Stachion without a glance at us. I wasn't sure if he even registered that his master was dead or not.

With all traces of the night's events gone from the forest, Asuna and I made our way back to Suribus, which was a closer trip than Stachion at this point.

"......So sleepy......so tired......so hungry......"

As soon as we passed through the town gates, and the text reading SAFE HAVEN vanished, Asuna slumped against the pillar of the gate. Then she looked up at me and frowned.

"...What kind of an expression is that?"

"Oh...just that you said the kind of thing that I'd normally say first," I replied.

She looked at me for a few moments, aghast, then slumped even farther. "You know...I can't even bring myself to deny that slander. Let's just go to the inn..."

"Good idea," I said, checking out the main street, which was much quieter now.

If we'd proceeded through the abduction event as it was meant to go, without Morte's interference, we'd have been released in Stachion after a brief scuffle and stayed at the inn over there. Now that we were unexpectedly back in Suribus, we had to deal with the issue of the overbooked inn rooms that Argo warned us about.

"Uh…well…I don't think we're going to find two single rooms side by side…" I suggested warily.

Asuna blinked blearily at me and mumbled, "A two-bedroom suite is fine…That was the original idea, remember?"

That was, indeed, what we discussed, but it was mostly to protect against PK attacks, and now that Morte's group wasn't likely to strike again for a while, it didn't seem necessary for the next day or two. On the other hand, the man in the black poncho who was their ringleader didn't make an appearance this time, and the only lasting damage we did to them was mental and material, so there was no guarantee they wouldn't come back as soon as tonight.

"Got it. In that case…I think there was a good spot on the left bank of the river. Let's try that one," I suggested. Asuna mumbled an affirmative and stood up unsteadily. She reached out toward me, causing me brief panic when I thought she wanted to hold my hand. Instead, she grabbed the end of my belt, which stuck out of my coat.

So with Asuna on autopilot and allowing me to chauffer her around, I took us to a four-story building close to the north gate. It was an above-average inn for Suribus, and on top of it, all the rooms had balconies facing the river, giving it the best view in town.

The Jade and Kingfisher was about 80 percent full, probably because of its unassuming signage, and if we didn't care about being adjacent, we could've taken two single rooms. But Asuna, who was still clutching my belt, ordered the deluxe suite room without a moment of deliberation.

My partner seemed to be completely out of batteries. I pushed her up the stairs and opened the puzzle-free door to our room. A huge window straight ahead showed us the night view of Suribus. If we went on the balcony, we'd see the lights of the town reflecting on the river below, but Asuna just staggered into the center of the living room and glanced at the bedroom doors on opposite walls.

"…I'll take this one. Good night…" she said, yawning, and vanished into the room on the left. I heard the sound of her equipment being removed—and then silence.

I snuck up to the open door and saw Asuna, still in her regular clothes, facedown on the spacious bed. After a few seconds of hesitation, I entered the room and grabbed the edge of the sheet cover beneath her.

I very carefully pulled it to roll Asuna over—she was already fast asleep—so that she was faceup atop the sheets and pillows. Then I laid the blanket back over her, whispered "Good night," and left the room. After a moment, I decided to leave her door open.

Back in the living room, I exhaled.

It was, indeed, a deluxe accommodation. There was a very fancy set of furniture in the middle of the room, with a basket of fruit on the table between the sofas. I picked up a fruit that had the shape of a kiwi and color of a strawberry and took a bite. It had the texture of a banana, with a pineapple flavor.

As I ate, I reflected on the past.

When we stayed at a deluxe room in Zumfut on the third floor, there was a fruit basket there, too. I recalled Asuna hurling a fruit that tasted like a mix of apple, pear, and lychee at me—but even though it was only two weeks ago, I couldn't remember why she had done it.

And yet, I could distinctly recall the conversation we'd had there.

*If I'm ever more of a hindrance than a help, you'd better tell me,* Asuna had said as we were lying down on adjacent beds. Her reason for leaving the Town of Beginnings was so that she could be herself…not so she could have me protect her.

Since that day, Asuna had worked tirelessly to continue proving that statement true. She absorbed a massive amount of information about how the game worked, she got better at fighting, and she even got over her fear of dueling other players. All I taught her at the dark elf camp this morning were a few technical pointers and some tips about mind-set, and tonight she'd held her own against Morte's partner. If I was going to beat her in a duel at this point, I couldn't win with fundamental abilities alone. I'd need to use some kind of higher-level trick.

So worrying endlessly about exposing Asuna to danger was, in a way, an insult to her. But this knowledge didn't help me stop blaming myself.

I finished the fruit and opened up my inventory, scrolling through the items in order of acquisition until I spotted the name NAMNEPENTH'S POISON JAR (0). This was the little container of poison gas that had paralyzed Asuna and me, as well as saved us from danger, though it was now empty. I tapped the name and moved it to the head of my item list, fixing its location through a submenu. This way, I'd see the name every time I opened my inventory and be reminded of my bitter mistake.

In Aincrad, poison—especially the paralyzing kind—was an incredibly powerful weapon. Monster paralysis attacks could be avoided with knowledge and experience, but it was almost impossible to perfectly defend oneself against a malicious and clever player armed with it. If we continued fighting against this PK gang, they'd almost certainly put us in danger with paralyzing poison again. But at the very least, I wasn't going to let Asuna be exposed to that danger a second time. Never again.

I closed my window and started to reach for the button to remove all my equipment, but I thought better of it and physically removed my sword and sheath from my back. I drew the sword slowly to avoid making any noise and let the lamplight hit the flat of the blade. Despite the furious battle against Morte and the following slaughter of the muriquis, the thin Sword of Eventide shone as brilliant and clear as a mirror.

When I had executed Rage Spike at the center of Morte's chest, the sword had curled and twisted like a living object to pierce his heart—his critical point.

My two upgrades to Accuracy at the dark elf camp had kicked in and auto-aimed it...that was all. But in that moment, and the moment when it hit the core of the Annoying Wraith, the correction process felt very much like the will of the weapon itself. It wasn't that the sword was adjusting its path toward the weak point I was trying to hit, it was like the sword itself had spotted the point of least resistance and wanted to slice that exact target.

*…I'm overthinking this. It only feels weird because I've never used a weapon with an Accuracy upgrade on it before. Plus, it was a good thing it hit Morte in the heart and put the fear of a one-hit kill in him. Otherwise, they wouldn't have picked up and run away like that.*

I ran my fingers along the flat of the blade, then returned it to its sheath. This time, I hit the UNEQUIP button, and it vanished into my inventory, along with the coat.

Now that I was lighter, I glanced back at Asuna's room, thought for a moment, then entered the bedroom on the right. I pulled the top blanket off the bed and returned to the living room. I lay down on the sofa, which was slightly hard, and wrapped myself in the blanket. If I slept there, that put me in a slightly better position, just in case someone found a way to slip through the system and get into our room.

Asuna and I were equal partners, so acting like it was my duty to provide all the protection was pure arrogance. Still, if there was something I could do, I wanted to do it. I was sure that Asuna was watching over me in the same way, in some form I didn't even realize.

I tapped the table to bring up the room menu and turned out the lights. Closing my eyes, I thought I heard faint breathing from the other room through the blue-black darkness.

I whispered good night to her and felt my mind sinking somewhere very, very deep.

# 5

Unlike yesterday, the morning sky was gloomy and dark—though only visible through the strip of the outer aperture, of course. Our day's activities started with a bit of inventory housekeeping.

After we ate breakfast at the inn's restaurant, we returned to the fourth-floor suite and materialized the items earned over the previous day onto the table. The majority of items were materials of uncertain use dropped by the muriquis, like Spider Monkey Pelts and Fluffy Tails, but the real problem was what the late Cylon had dropped. The gold and jewels had been picked up by the Muriqui Snatchers before we retrieved them, so they were mixed among our cash now, but we weren't really sure if it was right to use or sell off the equipable items he'd dropped.

"…I wonder if Cylon has any family," Asuna murmured, lifting up a gaudy golden pendant.

I shook my head. "No…I don't recall there being a wife or children in that mansion of his."

"I see…But the bigger question is: Does this mean Cylon's just gone from Aincrad forever? Wouldn't that mean nobody else can start the 'Curse of Stachion' quest…?"

Again, I shook my head. "No…I doubt it'll come to that. My guess is that when he showed up at the hideout in Suribus, there was already a different Cylon back at the mansion in Stachion.

The one that Morte killed was just 'our' Cylon. I bet that it won't have any effect on other players who are going to start the quest after us."

Asuna pressed her fingers to her left temple and groaned, "Ugh...I just can't wrap my head around that idea. The instanced maps are hard enough, but having the same person in multiple places at once is just..."

"I know how you feel," I said with a laugh. I poured the pitcher of lemonade-ish juice into two glasses and gave one to her. I took a sip of the sugary liquid and continued, "During the 'Elf War' quest on the third floor, I'm pretty sure I mentioned how, in order to get the Anneal Blade on the first floor, you have to do a quest to gather medicinal ingredients from the forest for a sick girl. When she drinks the finished potion, she gets better, but only while you're in their cabin. Once another player enters the place to start the quest, they'll just see a sickly, suffering girl again. It's unavoidable, you see...People would be losing their minds if only the single earliest party could ever fulfill a certain quest. Still, there's just something jarring about it..."

"...Yeah, I know..."

Asuna took a sip of her juice, too. She puckered her lips, then sighed.

"...I feel like Cylon was in pain, too, deep down. He was Pithagrus's first apprentice, but his master said he couldn't inherit the title, so he got mad and killed him and then had to bear that secret for an entire decade, right? Plus, someone made off with the golden cube that had his bloody handprint on it, so he knew at least one person was aware of the truth...I have to believe that he was on edge for all ten of those years."

She was conjecturing as though Cylon were a real person.

As an NPC, I doubted he would feel any guilt at all because he wasn't programmed to. But thinking about it...Unlike in the beta, the current version of Aincrad featured multiple NPCs that had so much intelligence and emotion, they were almost indistinguishable from people. Kizmel, Viscount Yofilis…and perhaps Cylon, too.

Asuna leaned back against the sofa, exhaled, then continued, "I thought…that maybe at the end of the quest, Cylon would repent for his crime and accept his punishment…and perhaps even find forgiveness…but so much for that. Hey, Kirito."

"Hmm?"

"If we go back to Stachion, and we actually meet another Cylon in the mansion there, the quest won't actually continue where we left off, right?"

"No…I don't think it will. We didn't actually finish that crucial event, for one thing. I bet the quest log is still stuck partway through that…"

I had my inventory window open already, so I switched it to the quest tab and tapped on the 'Curse of Stachion' entry to make it the active quest. The final line of the quest read…

"Let's see…CYLON, LORD OF STACHION, HAS BEEN KILLED BY BANDITS. YOU MUST FIND THE PROPER PLACE TO USE THE TWO REMAINING KEYS."

We stared at each other in silence. Then we both looked down at the table. Among the various articles there were two keys, one made of gold and one of iron.

"Wh-wha…? Hang on, was Cylon getting killed part of the story of this quest…?" Asuna asked, but I shook my head several times.

"N-no, that's not possible. Morte and his buddy weren't NPCs, they were other players. It says they're bandits, but it's not like the *SAO* system was controlling them and making them do that."

"Then why does the quest log say that?"

"Um…ummmm…The only thing I can think of is that they considered the possibility that Cylon might be killed by another player when the event goes in between towns and prepared that message…maybe…?"

"Really?" she said, giving me a look of disbelief. "If they were going to go to that much trouble, couldn't they just make Cylon so super-tough that nobody could kill him?"

"Well, that's true…but then you'd have to wonder why someone who wasn't a fighter would be so strong, right? That's the kind of thing that *SAO* is really picky about…"

"True. I mean, they go to the lengths of printing the entire contents of all the books in the world, even if we can't read them," Asuna admitted. She put her glass of lemonade on the table and picked up both gold and iron keys. "This golden key is the one we found at the hideout, right? So…where do we use this iron key?"

"Dunno…The golden key goes to the dungeon underneath the lord's mansion, but I've never actually seen the iron one before…"

"Dungeon…? Is that where you find the golden cube?"

I wasn't sure if I should answer that question or not, but then I decided that since we'd already completely branched off the story line I was familiar with, it couldn't hurt, after all.

"Yeah," I admitted, "the one who took the cube from the site of Pithagrus's murder and hid it beneath the mansion was the former maid we talked to first. Her name was…Theano, I think. She was actually a puzzle genius herself, and Pithagrus wanted to make her his heir to the title."

"Oh, really…? But Theano saw Cylon murder Pithagrus, right? Why did she hide the murder weapon, rather than accusing him as a witness?"

"See, the thing is, Cylon and Theano were lovers."

"Oh, my…ooh, aah," Asuna murmured as she took this in, gazing at the keys in her hands. "Ten years ago…Cylon would be in his late thirties, and Theano would've been around twenty-five, I think. So maybe she didn't feel like accusing her lover of murder, but her conscience didn't allow her to stand by and do nothing…"

"That's about how it went, I think. Theano locked the golden cube beneath the lord's mansion, then placed the key to it in the hideout in Suribus. She wanted Cylon to admit to his sin and atone for it."

"…What do you mean?"

"The dungeon under the mansion is a string of super-hard puzzles, and you can't even get to the last part without a hint from one of the books in the study of the hideout. For ten years, Theano waited for Cylon to admit to his crime and seek her help. She was going to tell him the location of the second home if he did. In order to get back the golden cube, Cylon would need to study the books in the hideout as hard as he could and solve the puzzle dungeon. And in fact, that's the test that's meant to determine if you've got what it takes to inherit the title of puzzle king and lord of the mansion."

"Aha…but Cylon didn't attempt the test himself, he just kept hiring people to do it…"

"And paralyzing and abducting the people he hired, to boot," I noted.

Asuna let out a long breath. "If Morte hadn't interfered…what would've happened to us?"

"Cylon was going to lock us in the mansion dungeon to make us retrieve the cube for him. But Theano found out, and she would help us in the backstreets of Stachion, and from that point on, we'd work with her on the quest, in the main route…"

"Hmm. Maybe we should ask Theano what to do with this key, then," Asuna suggested, holding up the iron one.

I tentatively agreed. "That would be…the orthodox idea. We could also ignore Theano, use the golden key to go into the dungeon and get the cube on our own. But I can't predict how the story will proceed in that case."

"Well, no use wasting any time, then." Asuna straightened up with the keys still in hand, but I grabbed her sleeve and forced her back into a sitting position.

"Hang on. We still haven't finished the most important investigation."

"Huh? But the rest of this is Cylon's stuff, right? Wait, you're not going to *sell* them, are y—?"

"No, no, no, I'm not. Although I bet this gas mask would go for a pretty good sum…"

I briefly lifted the rather ugly leather mask Asuna had worn last night when she'd snuck up on the dagger user, then put it back on the table. Then I put all the equipment into the special hotel-room item storage, clearing off the table so I could materialize the dark metal throwing pick and the much-used dagger.

Asuna grimaced when she saw them. "Oh, right…You were very fixated on them. That reminds me, another one of them dropped for me."

"What?"

To my disbelief, Asuna opened her window and quickly produced a new pick. Laid side by side, it was clear that in color, texture, and curving hexagonal design, it was identical to the first. Although this was surprising, I quickly realized that the first pick of the set of three had missed me and vanished into the trees when Morte threw it. A Muriqui Snatcher must have picked it up, and when Asuna defeated it, the pick would've dropped into her inventory.

"Ooh, nice combo work, monkey and Asuna."

"That…doesn't sound like a compliment," she muttered, grimacing again. "But…hang on…" She put a finger to her cheek and remarked, "All the items we got from the muriquis went straight into our item storage, right?"

"Yeah," I said, wondering where she was going with this, but I found that I had no answer to her next question: "Then why did all of Cylon's items fall to the ground when Morte killed him…?"

"Uh…mmm……"

She had a very good point. We'd survived because Cylon dropped his Namnepenth's Poison Jar within breathing range of us. But shouldn't it automatically have gone into Morte's inventory?

"Well, there are two possibilities I can see. Either Morte had barely any space left in his inventory…or the rules for dropping items is different when a player kills another player or an NPC."

"…Morte's probably very high-level, so I have my doubts about the former."

"That's true. He's bound to be limited in space because he switches between sword and ax, but even then, I can't imagine that he planned to come attack us while being just under the weight limit. So it might be a special set of rules…but there's no way for us to test that out."

"How did it work in the beta?"

"I feel like it was the same as when hunting monsters…but I didn't PK, so I can't tell you for sure…If we run into Argo somewhere, we should ask her," I said, putting a hold on the topic of item drops and returning to the black pick on the table.

We'd gotten two of the three poisoned picks, but the real issue was where they'd come from. I prayed there would be a hint to the answer in the item properties and tapped one of them. Asuna and I leaned closer to read the information.

"Um…it's called a…Spine of…Sh…Shmargor…? I think?" she hedged.

"What does that mean?" I asked. I'd been feeling like I was using my partner as a walking English-Japanese dictionary, but Asuna didn't seem to be annoyed.

"Spine is probably like 'thorn' in this case. I'd assume Shmargor is a given name, but I've never heard of it in the real world or in Aincrad."

"Mmm…"

I continued reading. The attack and durability ratings were a bit higher than what you could buy at a store—but nothing shocking. The real issue was the special effect below that.

"PARALYSIS (THREE): WHEN THIS WICKED SPINE STRIKES, IT CONFERS A LEVEL-TWO PARALYZING POISON EFFECT. THE POISON WILL WEAR AWAY AFTER THREE USES…Wow, level two? We haven't even gotten level-one paralyzing poison yet. That means a level-one cure potion from an item store probably won't even work on this."

"Then…what can you do?"

"Either level up the Mixing skill so you can craft level-two cure pots or use a Purify Crystal...but..."

Asuna's brow knotted. "How much proficiency do you need to craft level-two potions?"

"About one hundred, I think."

"Ugh."

That reaction was so perfectly in line with what *I* would say that I couldn't help but side-eye her. Asuna recognized what she'd done and turned a bit red, stammering, "A-and we're not getting any crystal items yet at this stage. So at the moment... there's no way for us to counteract the paralysis of this pick?"

"Um...well..."

The primary way to undo damaging or paralyzing poison was by using potions or crystals, but that wasn't the entirety of it. Among the seemingly unlimited types of food and drinks of this world were some with debuff-curing effects, and there was a good variety of material items that provided curative and healing benefits when used on their own. Then there were armor and accessories that boosted poison resistance, and...

My mind was completely off on this tangent when Asuna sucked in a sharp breath. She'd been reading the flavor text at the bottom of the properties window.

"Oh..."

"Wh-what is it?"

"THE SUNKEN ELF GENERAL N'LTZAHH FACED THE DREAD DRAGON SHMARGOR AND CUT OFF EVERY LAST ONE OF ITS SPINES, WHICH DRIPPED WITH DEADLY POISON," she recited, as I followed the text. Apparently Shmargor was a dragon with poisonous spines. But that wasn't the crazy part.

The "sunken elf" was clearly referring to Fallen Elves. And the individual named General N'ltzahh was someone Asuna and I had witnessed in person.

"H...hang on. You mean this pick is a spine that General N'ltzahh chopped off a dragon?"

"That's what it says here..."

"B-but…why…?"

I had to pause there to get down the rest of my lemonade. "Why does Morte have something like that?"

"You don't think…he actually defeated General N'ltzahh…do you?" Asuna wondered.

I thought it over and shook my head. "No…I can't believe that. You saw the general's color cursor, didn't you?"

"……Yeah." Her cheeks went paler than usual.

We had witnessed General N'ltzahh in the Fallen Elf base hidden deep in the submerged dungeon on the fourth floor. I was level 16 at the time, and his cursor had looked pure black to me. I wasn't taken by even an instant's desire to leap out of my hiding spot and challenge him to a fight. Even now, ten days later and level 19, I was certain that if I'd done so, both I and Asuna would've been dead in less than a minute.

The Fallen Elf had been surrounded by an aura cold as ice, and even expert player-battlers like Morte and the dagger user wouldn't stand a chance against him. In other words, if they were tough enough to beat N'ltzahh, they could've easily killed us both without needing to take advantage of that paralysis event.

"If anything…they'd either have to sneak into the Fallen Elf hideout and steal them, or they got a very rare drop from one of the lower Fallen Elves—the kind we were fighting…I think…"

I myself wasn't certain about this at all. I decided to tap the dagger next to the picks. When I read the properties that appeared, my voice caught in my throat.

It was called the Dirk of Agony. Its special bonuses included better poison and frost resistance, and a low chance of causing bleeding damage to any target. The flavor text described it as "a dagger given as a prize from the Fallen Elf Commander."

"…A Fallen Elf prize?" I muttered. Asuna pushed my head out of the way with her own to read the text, and she was similarly shocked.

"Does this mean…it was a quest reward?"

"…"

I didn't have an immediate answer for her question. The item description didn't suggest any other interpretation, but if true, it would mean the dagger user received a quest from the Fallen Elf Commander, finished it, and got this dagger as a reward.

And if that was the case, then Morte's poison picks weren't stolen from a Fallen Elf, either, but they were likely given to him. It was one thing if it was a quest that could only be performed once, but in the off chance that it was a reward for a repeatable vanquishing or gathering quest...that would mean the paralyzing picks we'd worked so hard to steal were in practically limitless supply.

"Hey, Asuna—" I said, right at the exact same instant that she said, "Say, Kirito..."

We each used our eyes to motion the other to start, until Asuna, who was slightly less patient than I was, finally gave in and continued, "Well...I'm curious about the Stachion quest, but for now, I think it's smarter to investigate these picks a little more."

"I was just about to say the exact same thing," I said, which brought a bit of a smile to her lips before they tightened up again.

"If they can keep getting these weapons, as many as they want, that's major trouble. They might not only go after us, and we'd have to make sure that every last player fighting out in the wilderness has resistance against paralysis..."

"I completely agree," I said, "but like I mentioned before, we have very few options for dealing with level-two paralysis poison as it stands...so I think we should ask about that, too."

"Ask...whom?" Asuna wondered.

I gave her a sly grin. "A knight who would know something about the Fallen Elves and poisons."

The circular map of the sixth floor of Aincrad was split into five equal slices by steep lines of mountains, with a star-shaped lake in the center.

Stachion and its neighbor Suribus were in the northeast slice, and the labyrinth tower was in the adjacent southeast area, but the rocky mountains in between were so tall they nearly reached the underside of the seventh floor and blocked all passage.

Therefore, players needed to go around the floor in counter-clockwise fashion. The mountains were about a hundred yards wide at their base, and the dungeons that served as the passage-way were fairly short. But they were packed with annoying puzzles in each room, with a mid-boss waiting at the exit of each area.

The DKB and ALS, the two main guilds on the frontier, had switched from Stachion to Suribus on the very first day of the floor. After half a day of leveling and updating equipment, then a good rest at the puzzle-less inn, they were now planning to tackle the cave in the adjacent northwest area—at least, according to the message I got from Agil, leader of the Bro Squad.

At the time of that message, Asuna and I had been eating breakfast at the restaurant and planning to go back to Stachion before noon to finish the multi-part quest, after which we'd head for the northwest area. But because of the weapons Morte and his friend had dropped, our priorities had changed. We put our stuff away, checked out of the Jade and Kingfisher, and headed for the dungeon at the very south end of the area.

Although we left late and encountered a couple monsters along the road, the two of us were still faster than a full raid party of several dozen, so we could still see three groups milling outside the dungeon entrance in its deep valley by the time we got there.

"Darn, I was hoping they'd have cleared out the dungeon already, so we could just walk right through it," Asuna grumbled as she waited in the shade of the trees.

I considered this and suggested, "Wouldn't it be the same thing if we wait for them to go in, then sneak after them as they go?"

"There's a huge difference between 'We rushed but didn't make it in time' and 'We chose not to rush to make it there.' Plus, Agil's group is over there already."

Indeed, resting outside the dungeon were the eighteen members (in three parties) from the blue-clad DKB, another eighteen from the green-dressed ALS, and the four members of the Bro Squad who wore varying armor but held exclusively two-handed weapons. At the end of Agil's message, he'd said *If you have time, you can help us get through the dungeon*, so the thought of complaining about our own problems made me feel guilty.

"All right, I guess we should go," I said, straightening up and patting Asuna on the back. We headed into the narrow crevice that led to the dungeon. As we walked past the sheer rock wall with its odd relief carvings, I made sure to step as loudly as possible to announce my entrance—and then waved to the Bro Squad, who were closest to us, huddled around a small campfire.

"Yo—hey, guys," I greeted.

"Good afternoon, Agil, Wolfgang, Lowbacca, and Naijan," added Asuna.

The tough guys greeted us in return, although they only smiled at Asuna.

Silently cursing them, I sat down next to Agil. A quick glance down the way showed me that Kibaou's ALS and Lind's DKB were watching us with disgruntled expressions. I gave them a two-finger salute and turned back to the fire.

Unlike the real world, you didn't need to know anything to start a fire here, but finding high-quality logs for fuel was surprisingly difficult. There were fallen branches all over in the wooded areas, but if you wanted to make a good fire, you had to tap them to make sure their item name was Dead Tree Branch. A Living Tree Branch or Damp Branch would produce lots of smoke and a weak, unstable flame. They sold bundles of good firewood at the general store in town, but these were quite heavy and took up space, so you couldn't lug many around.

But thanks to the overall high Strength stat of the Bro Squad, they had plenty of carrying capacity, and they were using nice, store-bought logs. A metal tripod was set up over the fire, with a kettle hanging from the top and emitting the scent of tea.

"How long is this break lasting, Agil?" Asuna asked. The

man said it would be about ten minutes, so I judged I had just enough time and opened my menu to pull out a stash of sweet potatoes—the proper item name was Ichthyoid Potato—I'd been keeping since the fourth floor. I tossed three into the fire.

These food items were around in the beta, too, but they were originally sold off at bargain prices, probably because it was the half-fish monsters who dropped them. Since the fourth floor in the beta was a place of dry, dusty canyons, the presence of fishy creatures made them even creepier.

But once people found out that cooking them in a campfire made them tastier than any store-bought sweets, the price shot through the roof, and there was a potato rush as players slaughtered the half fish for their starchy loot. Information wasn't getting around as quickly in the current form of Aincrad, so I made a mental note to head back down to the fourth floor and stock up soon.

The next thing I knew, it had been five or six minutes, and a sweet smell was issuing from the campfire.

Asuna and the Bros paused in their chitchat, nostrils twitching, but I let the sweet potatoes sit in the fire as long as possible—the moment just before they got burnt for good was when they tasted best—and with perfect timing, I pulled out my sword and jabbed three quick times into the fire.

Sparks flew with the disturbance, but when I pulled out my sword, there were three perfectly cooked sweet potatoes skewered on its end. All five teammates held out their hands in silence, so I cut each of the potatoes in half and handed them out.

The green-tea-style liquid that Agil had brewed went very well with the half-fish potato. My hometown of Kawagoe in Saitama Prefecture was a well-known area for sweet potatoes, and I'd eaten them all the time since I was a kid. Therefore, I was both picky about the taste and texture as well as a bit tired of eating them, but even digital, I would give these sweet potatoes at least ninety-five out of one hundred.

The potato halves soon vanished into virtual stomachs, and six contented sighs escaped in unison. Wolfgang, who was planning to open a steak house on the second floor in the future, asked me where to get them. To avoid disillusioning him with the facts, I simply said, "I'll sell them to you for cheap," and finished my tea. The Bro Squad had surely fought some of the half-fish monsters in the fourth-floor labyrinth tower, but the Ichthyoid Cultivators that dropped the potatoes didn't appear alone, and they ran away once they got down to 50-percent HP, so the only reliable way to beat them was to use a major skill at the right moment.

Thirty seconds before the end of the break, the campfire was tidied up, and Agil let us into his party. The Bro Squad was just four members at the moment, so Asuna and I could fit into the maximum of six, but sooner or later they'd get more members, and we couldn't assume there'd always be a place for us. It was occurring to me that I'd need to think about what to do when we inevitably got bumped out of the raid group...when Asuna sidled up next to me with a question out of nowhere.

"Hey, Kirito. How does a player with an orange cursor get it back to green again?"

"Eh?"

Why would she ask that now?

I blinked but soon understood where she was going with it:

Morte and his comrade had slipped into the ALS and DKB by hiding their identities, and they were using various tricks to pit the guilds against each other. By the time I saw through their scheme on the third floor, Morte had already left the guild, but my guess was that the dagger user was still in the ALS.

But yesterday, he had attacked the NPC assisting Cylon, turning his color cursor orange. So he couldn't enter any town, and it would make it very difficult for him to meet his guildmates. That meant if there was any player among their ranks who had abruptly vanished last night or who was still among the group with some excuse for why he was orange, that was our man. But only if he hadn't gotten his cursor back to green at some point over the course of the night.

"To go from orange back to green, you need to complete something called an 'Alignment Recovery' quest. I don't know exactly how it works, but if your cursor turns orange, you'll occasionally come across NPC travelers or wanderers in the wilderness, and they'll give you a kind of trial quest...I think," I murmured, not entirely sure of my memory on the matter.

Asuna pondered this. "Is that something you can do in a night?"

"Apparently the difficulty and length of the quest changes depending on your crime. Stealing something cheap from an NPC might not need a very long quest, but if you attacked or killed someone, that would be much more serious. And if you commit the same crime again, the second time, the quest is harder than the first, and the third time is harder than the second. I seem to recall people saying that if you PKed about five players in the beta, it was essentially impossible to be restored to green again."

After all that, I realized I hadn't actually solved Asuna's concern, so I added, "I don't know how much it would take to repair the dagger guy's alignment, to be honest...Plus, he attacked the big man, but he didn't kill him..."

"Yes...and another problem is that only half of the ALS is here..."

"I kind of doubt they'd take us seriously if we explained the truth, too..."

We were interrupted from our hushed conversation by a loud, booming voice coming from the dungeon entrance.

"Hey, if you wanna tag along, yer welcome! But if you join the raid, you gotta follow our commands!"

It was a voice I'd never mistake for anyone other than the leader of the ALS with the morning-star hair spikes, Kibaou. I flashed him an okay sign, and he snorted and turned back to the entrance. Among his three parties were some familiar faces: Okotan the halberdier and Liten the full-plate girl who had helped us with the last boss fight. They made little motions to catch our attention, and Asuna and I bowed back.

Clearly, it had been decided that the ALS would take the lead on this dungeon, as DKB's Lind, Shivata, and Hafner led their parties behind the other guild without a word of complaint, and the Bro Squad, with their two extras, brought up the rear in similar fashion.

Kibaou confirmed that all parties were in order and boomed, "Let's get through this place an' eat lunch at the next town!"

The ALS members cheered heartily—the rest of us at half the volume—and the forty-two-man group of conquerors headed into the dungeon that split the mountain range.

In less than twenty minutes, we were infighting.

The dungeon itself was very simple, made up of large rooms and the hallways that connected them. We cleared out the ten Living Statue monsters that appeared in the first chamber without much trouble.

The problem arose when we reached the puzzle lock on the door at the back of the room.

It looked like a sliding puzzle—in Japan, these are often called daughter-in-the-box puzzles—with blocks in large, medium, and small sizes that could be slid around. To beat the puzzle, you had to maneuver the large block placed at the very top of the puzzle all the way to the exit at the bottom. But while in the beta test there was one large block, four vertical blocks, one horizontal block, and four small blocks—a fairly easy orthodox example—the puzzle on the door now was longer—with eight small blocks in total.

Naturally, it was Kibaou who confidently made the first attempt. But after five minutes, and at least three hundred moves, he was nowhere nearer to solving it, and Lind, who was getting tired of waiting, suggested he give up and let someone else try. Kibaou yelled at him to stay out of it, and eventually the DKB and ALS had taken sides across the room in a glaring contest.

"Well...this certainly looks familiar." Asuna sighed in exasperation as she leaned against a distant wall. "Say, isn't there a simple and reliable way to solve that, like with the fifteen puzzle?"

"Unfortunately, there isn't...I remember that the shortest

solution to the original version was eighty-one moves, but this one has four extra blocks on it. I don't think I'd be able to step in and do it smoothly."

As we spoke, Kibaou was busy clattering the metal blocks as he slid them back and forth. But he was merely finding himself back in the same spots he'd been in minutes earlier, and he was getting no closer to a solution.

"By the way, Kirito, the puzzles in Stachion were some curse from the lord of the town, right? We didn't do that quest, so I don't know the fine details," said Agil, joining our conversation.

I looked up at his craggy face and nodded. "Someone died at the lord's manor, and now the place is cursed."

"Then why are there puzzles in this dungeon that's miles away from the town? There wasn't a single one in Suribus."

"...That's a good point."

I'd always known the sixth floor as the one with puzzles, so I never thought further about it, but now that he mentioned it, if the curse didn't even extend to Suribus, it didn't make much sense that it was afflicting this dungeon farther away. In fact, the puzzles spread to the south area across the lake and to the labyrinth tower as well, and I didn't recall anything in the beta that rationalized this.

*Well...it's all just a setting someone made up*, I concluded lamely, and I was gauging if I should say it aloud when someone's voice interrupted me.

"Hey, you just reset it to the beginning!" Lind bellowed, drawing our attention.

Indeed, on the massive sliding puzzle that opened the stone door, the large block that was meant to escape from the bottom of the puzzle was back to its starting position at the top. As he fiddled with the long vertical blocks below it, Kibaou grunted, "When you get stuck, you start over! It's common sense!"

"You just admitted you got stuck! So let someone else have a go!"

"I didn't say that!"

"Yes, you did!"

Exasperated with their bickering, Asuna commented, "Sometimes I get the feeling that they're actually best friends."

"You might be right about that..."

"Oh, just go over there and solve the puzzle for them already, Kirito."

"L...listen, there's a whole extra row added to what was there before. I can't beat it with the moves I remem..."

But then I came to a realization: Yes, there was an extra row of blocks, but the difference was just four new single-size blocks at the bottom that were the most maneuverable type, so in fact, they could largely be ignored. All you had to do was get the large block down to the spot where it was originally supposed to go and then slip two of the small blocks around the sides of it, creating a path to the exit.

"Um..."

Asuna was grinning.

"...Well, I guess I'll give it a try."

Agil smirked.

Leaving the pair behind, I crossed the large chamber to the locked door. Kibaou and Lind both noticed my footsteps and turned to me, ready to object, but I held up my hands to cut them off.

"Listen, there's no trick to this puzzle other than memorizing the moves. I'll do this one, and if you can remember how I do it, then you should be able to do it in a snap if you come across the same thing."

The two clamped their mouths shut, then shared a quick glance. Lind nodded, while Kibaou turned his back on me.

"Well, if you say so, then I'm willin' ta let you try."

"Then if you'll pardon me..."

I approached the puzzle that Kibaou had just reset and started working on it, relying on memory. I'd said there was no trick to it other than memorization, but in general, the quickest method was to gather the long vertical blocks on either the left or right side, then eventually get them to take up the top rows.

Thankfully, I managed to inch the largest block downward without getting stuck, until it was at the original exit position. As I theorized, once the block was there, it only took a few moves to adjust the new blocks out of the way and slide that large block to the bottom spot.

"Ooooh," the crowd of players murmured, as the massive door sank into the floor, offering us passage into the hall beyond.

"Let's get movin'!" Kibaou said triumphantly, leading his guildmates through.

Part of my showing off was on Asuna's request, but there was another purpose for it, too. As the ALS passed, I casually began strolling with them until I could approach a mustachioed dandy in their back row.

"Hiya," I whispered to Okotan, the captain of the ALS's recruitment team. He glanced at me and murmured, "Nice work."

"Thanks. Listen…I hate to ask this out of the blue," I began, prompting a curious look from him, "but of the members originally slated to participate in this dungeon, did anyone drop out abruptly just beforehand?"

But the truth was that I was already expecting to hear a certain name as Okotan's answer.

The man who gave me the nickname of Beater after beating the first-floor boss, the man who tried to have Nezha crucified for his part in the weapon-upgrading scandal, the man who claimed Asuna and I were trying to monopolize the "Elf War" questline on the third floor, the man who stayed away on the fourth floor but accused me of trying to get the guild flag for myself at the fifth-floor boss, the man with the catchphrase "I know the truth"—the man named Joe. I'd found myself suspicious of him on a few separate occasions, and when he wasn't among the ALS members in this dungeon, my suspicions grew deeper.

The only things Joe shared in common with Black Hood Number Two were that they both used daggers and were about the same height. Number Two had his hood pulled low last night and also when I spotted him in the catacombs—and Joe always wore a leather mask that hid his face, so neither of them actually showed off his features. Their high-pitched voices were similar, too, but masks could change that, so it wasn't a reliable detail.

But on the fifth floor, Kibaou had said to Joe that the information he'd brought about the guild flag was accurate. That meant that at the very least, Joe had access to beta information, which *could* have come from Morte, who was a tester. The ALS had a few other dagger users, and much like Morte, there was no guarantee that Number Two wasn't switching his primary weapon while he was working with the ALS—but if Okotan mentioned Joe's name, my suspicion would turn almost to conviction.

"Well…" Okotan started, seemingly without any suspicion and with his eyes darting up to the left, where the list of his raid members would be. He shook his head. "No, nobody changed their plans. Everyone who signed up at yesterday's meeting is present here."

"Oh…I see," I said, without any visible reaction. On the inside, however, I was taken aback.

Morte and his pal must've known, in planning last night's attack, that they would become orange players because of it. Even if their plan was to complete an "Alignment Recovery" quest overnight to get back to green, Number Two had lost his special Dirk of Agony in the act of saving Morte. If he hadn't thrown it to distract me, I would have smashed the smoke bomb away with my sword in the instant before it exploded.

Losing the powerful weapon he'd received from the Fallen Elf would be a major blow to his battle power, and such a loss might affect his ability to complete the recovery quest before morning. I had assumed that if Number Two was Joe, he would come up with some excuse for why he suddenly couldn't take part in today's activity—but it turned out that Joe was never scheduled to be here.

I needed to get as much information as I could while I had the opportunity. "Um, what time of day did you have that meeting, exactly?" I asked.

"It was after dinner, so probably around eight thirty in the evening," Okotan said. At last, he seemed to find something suspicious about my questioning. "Why would you want to know something like that?"

"Er...well...Late last night, we saw someone who looked like they were in the ALS fighting out in the woods, and they were struggling. I was just concerned, that's all..."

I knew it was a weak explanation, but in fact, I wasn't really lying—I just wasn't going to reveal that his opponents were me and Asuna.

Okotan took this at face value, however; in fact, he even bowed a bit. "Oh, I see. Thank you for your concern. I didn't hear anything about any members being in trouble last night, so I don't believe there was a problem."

"Oh, good," I replied, pondering this.

If the meeting was at eight thirty, it would've been after nine when they finished. The attack on us happened after nine; if our second attacker was, in fact, Joe, he couldn't have been at the meeting.

I wanted to know if Joe was there or not, but asking as much would be fishy at this point. And even if Joe wasn't at the meeting, that merely increased my suspicion without giving me any hard evidence.

If only I could figure out the reason why Joe wouldn't be taking part in this dungeon run today, when he'd been in every single boss fight thus far...

"Yo, the next room's up ahead! All members prepare fer combat!" Kibaou shouted from the head of the line. His ALS followers brandished their weapons. I decided there wasn't much point trying to talk further and thanked Okotan before I drifted back.

Once the DKB had filed past and I was in the rear again, Asuna zeroed in on me. "What were you talking with Okotan about?"

"I was asking if any of their members backed out from this at the last minute."

Asuna instantly understood where I'd been going with that. She leaned closer. "And...?"

"Sadly, he said there weren't any."

"……Oh…I guess it wasn't going to be that easy to catch him by the tail…"

"Yeah. At this rate, we should keep our wits about us all throughout the day."

"What do you mean?"

I leaned over. "The truth is that it's not actually too hard to cover up the reason you went orange. He could have said he used an area attack that accidentally hit an NPC—and gotten his guildmates to help him do the 'Alignment Recovery' quest. The reason he didn't is probably because he considered the possibility that the attack last night wouldn't work. He could trick his guild-mates, but if you or I survived and learned that someone in the ALS turned up orange, we could confirm that he was our PKer… And if they're savvy enough to plan that carefully, they could have decided that we'd let our guard down, thinking they won't attack again the next day, making us easier targets this time."

"…When you put it that way, it seems likely. So assuming that we'll be watching our backs more carefully from now on," Asuna contemplated, leaning in very close with an angry glare, "I'd like a correction to your quote just now about 'if you or I survived.'"

"Wha…?"

"Why would you think that if one of us was killed, the other one would run away? Say it again, but correctly: 'if you *and* I.'"

"O-okay…"

I wasn't planning to abandon Asuna and run away, of course, but I did think it possible that I might need to use myself as a shield to help her get away…and if I dared to suggest it out loud, I'd get more than an angry glare in return. So I agreed with her and started to correct myself—when I heard a crude whistle from behind us.

"Things are getting steamy over here!"

"They're melting the North Pole!" taunted Lowbacca and Nai-jan of the Bro Squad. Almost instantaneously, Asuna and I were no longer touching shoulders and leaning our heads in, but keeping a healthy distance.

I couldn't help but think, *I didn't taunt Shivata and Liten that way, because I told myself that being in ninth grade meant I was too old for that!*

We managed to get through four of the large rooms—each of the door puzzles being the same type, in increasingly complex arrangements, but we got through them all despite Kibaou and Lind's bickering—until the final chamber greeted us with a huge, vine-plant boss. It rapidly grew pods that hurled explosive peas at us, until Agil and Lowbacca charged in with their battle-axes to cut it free from the roots, at last.

I didn't get the Last Attack bonus, as I was busy dodging the explosives, but according to Agil, all he got for it was a huge bunch of peas. With great sympathy, I suggested that maybe they'd be sweet if boiled. Once out of the dungeon, we split off from the rest of the frontliners.

The ALS, DKB, and Bro Squad headed over the western horizon toward the faint silhouette of the next town, but Asuna and I had another destination in mind: The dark elf fortress on the sixth floor was located in this northwest slice of the map.

"...I don't think there's much use in complaining about the map design of Aincrad at this point," Asuna said after a few minutes of walking off the path through the wilderness, "but when there's only a single line of mountains between us and the first area, it really shouldn't be *this* different."

"No arguments from me," I replied.

The northeast area that contained Stachion and Suribus was mostly thick forest, like the third floor, but adjacent to it on the map, the northwest area was burnt-red desert, just like a western movie. There was no verdant plant life on this rolling terrain, just weathered rocks and the oddly shaped cactus here and there. When a particularly strong breeze started, it kicked up sand into little whirlwinds that impeded your vision.

Hunger and thirst couldn't kill you in Aincrad, but in the real world, you'd never set foot in a place like this without more than a few bottles of water. Our destination was near the aperture directly north, after a hike of about two and a half miles. And there was no path to take, so we had to avoid dried riverbeds and rocky outcroppings along the way, while battling the many monsters that appeared.

Fortunately, my partner failed to find the giant scorpions, giant centipedes, and giant camel spiders to be quite as icky as the astral monsters, despite the fact that most girls would absolutely hate them. And just when my inventory was getting close to full with unappetizing ingredient items like scorpion tails and camel spider jaws, I finally hit the milestone of level 20.

"Yahoo!"

The moment the level-up light surrounded me, I raised my right fist and leaped into the air in celebration. Asuna, who had reached level 19 not that long ago, backed away a foot.

"S-since when did you start acting like that?"

"I also did this when I reached level six and level twelve," I insisted.

At last, Asuna recognized the occasion. "Oh, so you got another skill slot...In that case, some congratulations are indeed in order."

"Yahoo!"

"Sure, sure, sure. So what are you taking for your fifth skill?"

"Mamma mia!" I cried, realizing I was getting a bit carried away just as my partner abruptly hit me with an ice-cold stare. I cleared my throat in embarrassment.

"Currently, I've got one-handed longswords, martial arts, Search, and Hiding...so I think I'll either go with Throwing Knives or Sprint..."

"I recommend Sprint," she said. "It cuts down on movement time, and it just feels good to run."

"Yeah, I like that skill, but..."

I considered that it had been a month since we started working together, and that it was probably okay to ask by now, but even still, I felt hesitation.

"Say, Asuna…you've got rapiers and Light Metal Armor and Tailoring and Sprint, and what's the other one?"

At level 19, Asuna only had four slots still, but thanks to the ultra-megaton rare item that was likely unique among the entire world, the Crystal Bottle of Kales'Oh, she could effectively use a fifth skill. From what I knew, she was using the bottle to switch between Tailoring and Sprint, so whatever she had in the final slot had been a mystery all this time.

Asuna blinked three times at the question, and to my surprise, she looked up and away from me, pursing her lips. That only made me more curious, but I never would have predicted her reply.

"Um…it's a secret. I don't want you to get mad at me."

"H-huh?! Get mad? …Me? Hang on, I'm not going to get mad…Though, I mean, whatever skills you choose are your own business…"

"The teachers who say that are the ones who get the angriest."

"T-teachers…"

*Well, she might be right about that. But I'm still not a teacher.*

Asuna took advantage of my silence to jab her finger at me. She continued, "We're not talking about me right now. I was asking you what skill you're going to take."

"Uh, r-right…Well, I think it'll either be Throwing Knives or Sprint, but I'll hold off for now…"

"I see. Well, let's keep moving," she commanded, turning her gaze to the north without chastising my lack of decisiveness. I guess she really didn't want to talk about her fifth skill.

For the last few minutes, we'd been walking in sandy canyons that reminded me of the American state of Utah—based on movies, not any personal experience, of course. The terrain was monotonous but complex here, and consulting the map didn't tell you much except for which direction you were traveling, but the only way to reach our goal was to get through this natural maze.

As long as we knew the proper route, we could run straight there and avoid all the monsters, but even a beater like me, who'd only run the maze once several months ago, didn't have the lay-out memorized. We just had to keep pressing forward, slaughter-ing all the scorpions, centipedes, and Mongolian death worms that crawled out of cracks in the dusty canyon walls. The light trickling into the canyon was getting darker and thicker by the time we finally came across a sign of civilization.

Suddenly, the canyon floor was wider, and many stone pillars lined the way, with stone blocks placed like a bridge over the fine sand. There was a large gate ahead of us, atop which streamed a mul-titude of banners with a familiar insignia of scimitars and horns.

"…Wow, that is huge…"

Asuna was tiring from all the constant battle, but even she couldn't hide her reaction to the distant castle gate. Level-wise, she was still plenty strong for this area, but the combination of all these poisonous monsters and the wariness of fresh PK attempts had only amplified the mental toll.

We couldn't just stay on guard for these PKers all the time. We had to think of proactive ways to remove the threat they posed, I told myself as we headed over the stone bridge.

"Castle Galey up there is the largest of the dark elf fortresses. The building itself isn't as posh as Yofel Castle, but they've got a dining hall and a bath."

"Wait, you mentioned a bath?"

Asuna didn't jump into the air with a "*Yahoo!*" but the change in her expression suggested her energy meter had shot from 30 percent up to 70 or so. She picked up her pace, and I hurried to match her, eventually deciding I ought to elaborate.

"The thing is…the dining hall is great, but there's something about the bath that might be a problem…or might not…"

"……What is it?"

"Wellll, it's, uh, actually…public…"

Asuna didn't understand what I meant at first. She repeated "Public…?" a few times, then scowled. "Is this like the antonym of instanced? So it's not a space that's just for us? Other players can come in?"

"That's right. Out of all the dark elf spots, only the queen's castle on the ninth floor and Castle Galey up there are public...I'm guessing they found it difficult to have a whole bunch of these fortresses and castles all existing in the same space at the same time..."

"Well, Yofel Castle was plenty big, too. But I guess I can't complain...So your point is that other players might enter the dining hall and bath and stuff," she said. I could practically hear the effervescence of her energy meter decreasing, so I hastened to clarify.

"In theory, yes, but the only people who can pass through that gate are ones doing the 'Elf War' questline with the dark elf faction, who are at least as far along as we are. I don't think there's a single other player who qualifies at this point, so go ahead and bathe to your heart's content...I could even stand guard outside, like I did on the third floor..."

Asuna appeared to grapple with this idea but abruptly shifted into dead seriousness. "And the dark elf castle is definitely not a safe haven, right?"

I was briefly taken aback, and I glanced up at the gate, which was much closer now. The anti-criminal code that promised absolute protection over a player's HP and life was invisible, but there was *something* different about the air surrounding the castle when compared to human towns. I looked back at her and nodded.

"Yeah...I believe so. It's theoretically possible for Morte's gang to get inside and attack us somehow. But like I said, they'll need to be involved with the dark elf faction to do that. I don't think they had that much time to work with...and at the very least, it would be impossible for J—for the dagger user infiltrating the ALS."

Asuna's eyebrow twitched when I started to say the name, but her reaction didn't go beyond that. Her suggestion involved an unexpected character. "Do you think...Viscount Yofilis would tell us if we asked? Could he say if Morte or his friends were working for the dark elves?"

"Hmm..."

I came to a stop without realizing it, crossing my arms.

Eventually, I shook my head. "No…Yofel Castle is an instance, so Viscount Yofilis should exist in different states for each party working on his quests. According to *our* Viscount Yofilis, he'd probably say we're the only humans assisting the dark elves in their struggle."

"Oh…Once again, I have to say, I don't like that system," Asuna opined with a shrug. She turned to the tall castle gate. "We'd better be on guard in the castle, then. C'mon, let's go."

"Yeah," I agreed, and my partner and I crossed the last bit of the stone bridge to approach the huge gate, which appeared to be carved out of one single, giant rock formation.

In all previous camps and forts, there had always been guards at the entrance, but there was a special reason that Castle Galey's elves almost never ventured outside. Instead, sharp voices issued forth from the bay windows atop the gate.

"Begone!"

"This gate does not open for the likes of humankind!"

These warnings were even harsher than those at Yofel Castle. But by holding high the Sigil of Lyusula ring that Viscount Yofilis gave me, I caused the guards at the bay windows to turn around and signal behind them. A clear, crisp bell began clanging from somewhere within the castle, and the gate slowly opened.

It would take nearly a full minute for the gate to open all the way, so once there was space enough for a person to get through, I prodded Asuna to go on, then followed after her. The instant we crossed the threshold, the gate reversed motion and began to rumble closed.

Asuna took three steps before she stopped and exclaimed, "Ooooh…!"

Castle Galey was built—more like sculpted—out of a circular basin over six hundred feet across. The three-story castle curved along the inside walls of the basin, but rather than being built of stone or wood, it was carved directly out of the natural rock formation like some ancient ruin.

Surrounding the castle in a C shape from east to west along the north side was an open area covered in tile mosaics, with dark elf guards and servants quietly coming and going. I didn't see any players at the moment.

Standing in the center of this open space was one massive hardwood tree. The desert and canyons we'd walked through to get here featured no plants aside from brown cacti, but the branches of this tree burst with vivid green leaves. A natural spring welled up with crystal-clear water at its roots, sparkling golden where the sun dripped through the branches.

Near the base of the tree was a large hollow knot, and if I squinted, I could see a faint, pulsing blue light inside it. When Asuna noticed it, she whispered, "Oh…is that…a spirit tree…?"

"Yeah. There's a spirit tree in the castle here."

The spirit trees were like teleporters that the dark elves and forest elves used to get from floor to floor, much like the gates we players had. But while our teleport gates could always be found in the biggest town on any floor, many of the spirit trees were placed far from any elven fort or castle, which I found curious at first.

Apparently, the spirit trees had a life span and grew anew every hundred years or so, but even the elves didn't know where they would sprout. The spirit tree on the sixth floor, however, was an outlier in its longevity and had been living for centuries even at the time they built Castle Galey around it.

I was explaining all this background information to Asuna when the door on the west wing of the castle opened loudly. Suddenly, Asuna's face burst into a brilliant smile.

"Asuna! Kirito!"

Greeting us and rushing over was a female knight wearing black-steel armor and a dark cloak, with a curved saber on her left hip. Her skin was a brilliant brown, and her short-cropped hair was grayish-purple.

Asuna walked forward and threw her arms wide. The knight leaped into them and circled her hands around the fencer's back. After more than five seconds of this embrace, she turned to me with open arms. I'd been going in for a handshake, so I had to stifle my shyness and accept her bear trap. Somewhere in my

head was the mysterious statement that *It's through heavy metal armor, so it's okay.*

The knight's embrace lasted another five seconds before she let go, stepped back, and clapped my shoulder. It was only three days ago that we parted, but it felt like it had been so much longer. I greeted the member of the Pagoda Knights Brigade of Lyusula, the beautiful dark elf who was our good friend.

"Kizmel, it's good to see you."

"It is indeed, Asuna and Kirito. I'm glad you've come...It must have been difficult to cross this arid land on foot," she said.

Asuna beamed. "It was nothing, knowing we'd see you at the end."

"I'm happy to hear you say that. Please, come inside and clean off the dust of your journey...but only after you've paid your respects to the liege of the castle. I'm sorry to delay your rest..."

"No, if we're going to enjoy the hospitality here, we must show our appreciation," I said. Kizmel looked apologetic but proceeded to escort us across the open square.

Reflecting on it now, between the camp on the third floor, Yofel Castle on the fourth, and Shiyaya Village on the fifth, the dark elf NPCs had never been openly hostile to us, but they'd been standoffish in general. It seemed that the quests we'd been doing for them had begun to affect their attitude, because as with the camp when we visited yesterday, the various guards and servants we passed in the open area gave us polite salutes. It could've just been because we had the elite knight with us, but I returned the gestures all the same. We headed to the left of the spirit tree—to the front gate of the castle.

The main body of the castle was a story taller than the wings and jutted about fifteen or twenty feet above the cliffs that surrounded the basin. I visited this place during the beta, but I merely accepted the main quest and reported back when I was done, so I didn't have strong memories of it.

But when I passed through the guarded doors into the main hall, I couldn't help but join Asuna in her admiration.

The exterior of Castle Galey was carved from the reddish rock, with detailed design but a uniform texture that didn't convey the same beauty that Yofel Castle did. But on the inside, it had finely laid black-and-ivory tiles and no hint at all that it was some archaeological ruin. I felt as though the interior was decorated in a simpler fashion during the beta, so either Argus's designers put hard work into spiffing up the place, or the dark elves had.

We crossed the perfectly clean hall—not a speck of dust to be seen—and ascended the double-spiral staircase to the lord's office on the third floor. The castle's master, Count Melan Gus Galeyon, was the extremely rare elf who was large and hearty, with a splendid beard. But he did not possess the same humanity (elfanity?) as Viscount Yofilis, and his dialogue was rather generic as he welcomed us with a main quest and three sub-quests.

When we left his chamber, Kizmel joined us in exhaling with relief. I stared at her profile without realizing what I was doing, and she gave me a guilty smile. "I am of common birth. Since receiving the duty of recovering the hidden keys, I have had more interactions with nobles, but it is not something one gets used to."

"Ha-ha, I'm a commoner, too. I get nervous around important people. I don't know about Asuna, though."

I had suspicions that Asuna was quite a pampered rich girl—despite her propensity for instant violence—and the fencer gave me a jab to the side, sure enough. "Of course I'm an ordinary civilian, and yes, I get nervous!"

"Ha-ha-ha. You two get along so well. Well, let me show you to your room."

Kizmel placed a hand on each of our backs and pushed us west, down a windowless hallway. We soon reached a guest chamber on the third floor of the west wing. On the opposite wall from the door was a lattice window, through which the sun setting over the horizon—make that the outer aperture of Aincrad—was bright red.

"Ooh, it's such a lovely room!" exclaimed Asuna, doing a full turn at the center of it.

"It's a bit smaller than the guest room at Yofel Castle, I know,"

Kizmel began, "but it's actually the second-best in all of Castle Galey."

"No, it's not cramped at all! I bet you could fit five people on this sofa alone!"

Asuna was showing signs of furniture obsession. She undid her equipment and plopped herself onto a long, wood-framed sofa with an elegant curved design. Kizmel grinned, removed her saber, and sat next to her. I got rid of my sword and armor and sank into an armchair across from them.

The suite at the Pegasus Hoof, where we talked to Lind about the guild flag, had been quite deluxe, too, but the castle of a count was quite naturally a level or two above in terms of quality furnishing and plushness of cushions. It seemed like a waste that Asuna and I were the only players stopping at this castle...and then I realized I had something to confirm first.

"Listen, Kizmel."

"What is it?" asked the knight, who was reaching for the plate of fruit on the coffee table between us. I chose my words carefully.

"Well...are there any other humans aside from us at Castle Galey, do you know?"

Suddenly, the smile vanished from Asuna's face. But Kizmel simply said, "No, there aren't."

"Oh, I see. Sorry for being weird," I said, relaxing. I picked up a star-shaped fruit from the dish.

"But I have heard of other human swordsmen assisting the people of Lyusula," she continued. "Perhaps you will come across them someday."

I froze in an awkward position, fruit held just before my open mouth.

Nearly two months had passed since the start of this game of death—and over two weeks since we opened up the third floor—so it wasn't strange at all that there would be other players undertaking the "Elf War" quest on the dark elf side. But if that just happened to be Morte and his friends, there was no protection here at Castle Galey against their malice.

Morte slaughtered Cylon, lord of Stachion, without a moment's hesitation. So if they wanted to, they would try to do that to the dark elves in this castle...and to Kizmel, too. In pure fighting power, Kizmel was overwhelmingly stronger than them, but there was no overlooking the wicked creativity of a motivated PKer.

We would need to fulfill our purpose for being at this castle as quickly as we could, I decided. I made eye contact with Asuna, then tossed the fruit in my mouth and opened up my game window.

What I pulled from my item storage, which the elves called Mystic Scribing, were the double-sided dagger and the two throwing picks, which shared a certain kind of cruelty in their design. As soon as she saw them arranged on the table, Kizmel's face tightened.

"...Kirito...what are those...?"

"Um...we were attacked by two fellow humans last night. They dropped these weapons in the attempt..."

Kizmel was already on her feet. "You were attacked?!" she yelled. "Was it just attempted robbery, or...?"

"Uh...I think they were trying to kill us..."

"......My word...!!"

The dark elf's onyx eyes glowed with pale flames—or so it seemed to me. She stood up straight, grabbing the saber she'd left standing against the side of the sofa, and shouted, "If I were there, I would have lopped their heads from their shoulders! Kirito, Asuna, you must not return to your human towns! You must stay with me..."

"No, no, no, we're fine," I assured the furious elf, getting her to sit back down. I pointed at the weapons on the table again. "We managed to drive them off without suffering much dam...er, any wounds. But they're very persistent, so there's no question they're still out to get us. The problem is the weapons they were using... Especially these, which are poisoned throwing needles. Can you tell us anything about this, Kizmel...?" I finished, all in a single breath, sliding one of the picks over to the knight.

"......"

Kizmel stood her saber against the sofa and lifted the pick high over her head, so that it caught the light from the window.

"…This isn't steel. It was fashioned from the spike of some living thing," she said.

Asuna leaned forward and tapped the other pick. She read the flavor text on its item properties out loud. "Kizmel, these human words say, THE SUNKEN ELF GENERAL N'LTZAHH FACED THE DREAD DRAGON SHMARGOR AND CUT OFF EVERY LAST ONE OF ITS SPINES, WHICH DRIPPED WITH DEADLY POISON…"

"N'ltzahh…Shmargor…?!" she repeated, rising again and initially hurling her hand with the pick away from her, before she regained her composure and placed the weapon on the table. She gave us both a look, then began to speak in an officious tone.

"…Shmargor is an evil dragon spoken of in elven legend. Long in the past, when the elves and humans and dwarves still lived on the earth, a wicked little snake snuck past the priestess and climbed the black Holy Tree to take a bite of the single fruit that grew at the tip of one of its branches. The snake gained eternal life, but it was cursed so that everything that entered its mouth turned to poison. Every time it ate, the snake suffered and died, only to come back to life through the fruit's holy power. After several centuries, the snake had evolved into a massive, ugly poison dragon that attacked towns and villages. But the human hero Selm defeated it, and it fled to the land of ice far to the distant north…"

Kizmel's rich voice faded out, prompting both me and Asuna to exhale. Her smooth and lyrical delivery was so pleasant to listen to, we wanted to ask her to tell us more, even though we knew she couldn't.

"…Hmm, that's kind of a sad story…I doubt the snake wanted to bite the Holy Tree's fruit out of malice…" Asuna said, shaking her head.

Kizmel nodded deeply. "The fruit of the Holy Tree is said to give eternal life, and its sap provides invulnerable flesh. Many tragic tales revolve around such fruit. There is this story, for example:

At the end of the Month of Holly, which humankind designates as December, there is a holy sage tasked with the duty of giving gifts to children. One year, he learned that the gift he was to give to a sickly little human girl was actually a piece of the Holy Tree's fruit. Unable to stifle his curiosity, he opened the present box and found an unbearably gorgeous crystal. The sage desired this crystal, and of all the thousands of children, he only failed to deliver that one little girl's gift. Without the protection of that crystal, the girl did not live to see the new year as she was meant to, and so the holy sage went mad, cursed to wander forever through a night that never ends..."

"...Do the other stories have similar endings?" Asuna asked.

Kizmel shrugged. "Most of them do. The gifts of the Holy Tree are not to be coveted."

"And from what I remember, the Fallen Elves were banished because they tried to harvest the sap of the Holy Tree," I interjected, which caused Asuna to gasp.

"Oh, right! The Fallen Elves were sent to the far north, too. So it would make sense that he encountered Shmargor up there...But wait, does that mean General N'ltzahh has been around since before Aincrad was created...?"

Kizmel frowned in silence while we talked, so I cautiously asked her, "Um, in fact...how many years ago did Aincrad come into being...?"

"...Actually, we royal knights do not know the details. As I believe Lord Yofilis told you, only Her Royal Majesty possesses all the legends surrounding the Great Separation and the six sacred keys. All we are told is that this floating castle was created long in the past."

She paused for a moment there, brushing the clasp of her cloak before continuing, "However, I have heard that Her Majesty and the forest elf king are very long-lived. So perhaps the man who leads the Fallen is equally ancient. Not that he frightens me."

That was a heartening attitude, but I didn't want Kizmel to end up fighting General N'ltzahh. I had no doubt of her skill as a knight, but even remembering the sight of N'ltzahh up close left me short of breath. He would be worse than anything we'd faced so far, including the five floor bosses.

Though Kizmel couldn't have known what I was thinking, she fixed me with a long look from her dark eyes and reached for the table again. This time, she picked up the black dagger that Number Two had dropped—the Dirk of Agony.

Unlike with the pick, Kizmel merely gave this a once-over, then stated, "Indeed. This is a Fallen weapon."

"You can tell just by looking?" Asuna asked, wide-eyed.

The knight indicated the base of the thin blade. "Do you see the symbol carved faintly down here?"

"Huh?" I yelped. I felt ashamed that I hadn't noticed it when I examined the weapon at the inn in Suribus, but sure enough, just above the hilt, there was a very fine carving that glinted orange in the sunlight. The design was of two folding lines that created a pattern of three diamonds, but I had no idea what it meant.

"What is this...?" Asuna wondered.

"It apparently represents ice and lightning," Kizmel answered.

"Ohhh," cooed two humans in unison.

The dark elves had a scimitar and horn, the forest elves had a shield and longsword, and the Fallen Elves had ice and lightning. In a different game, you'd figure the Fallen were masters of ice and lightning magic, but sadly—well, luckily, really—there was no magic in *SAO*.

Kizmel put the dagger back on the table and crossed her slender arms over her chest. "These are, indeed, weapons of the Fallen. The same mark was on the blades of those we fought on the third and fifth floors. But I seem to recall that the sigils I saw were not simple carvings, but cast silver."

"Now that you mention it, I think that's right..." Asuna agreed, but I couldn't honestly remember. I found it hard to believe that an AI like Kizmel would be mistaken, so I moved on from there.

"You're saying...this dagger is cheaper than the weapons of the Fallen we've fought to this point?"

"I would say so, but that is not all of it. I suspect these are weapons given to collaborators of other races...Meaning that those human vagabonds who attacked you did not steal that dagger from a slain Fallen, but they were given them for their assistance."

"......"

Asuna and I had discussed that very possibility based on the flavor text of the Dirk of Agony this morning. I felt like Kizmel's statement turned that vague suspicion into almost verifiable truth.

Morte and his buddy had found a quest route that involved collaborating with the Fallen Elves, rather than fighting against them. So we ought to assume there would be a way to regain those highly deadly poisoned picks. If we were going to keep fighting them, we needed a way to counteract level-2 paralyzing poison as soon as possible.

I drew in a breath to explain this, but I was beaten to the punch.

"Do not worry. As I told you earlier, as long as I am at your side, no vagabonds will threaten you," Kizmel stated flatly. She patted Asuna's knee lightly and stood up.

"Uh, K-Kizmel, we're not..." I started to say, but she only sat back down to motion us to stand with her.

"Why don't we wash off the dust of your travel first? You must have taken on quite a bit of sand during your trip to this castle."

Those words turned Asuna's eyes into hearts—or more accurately, into the symbol for hot springs. Nobody would be able to stop her now.

I quickly stashed the weapons back in my inventory and hurried after the women.

When I visited Castle Galey in the beta, I took a tour of the building. A stint in the baths wasn't on the tour, but I did remember the location of the facilities.

But Kizmel didn't head to the second floor of the east wing, where I remembered it. She descended the stairs in the center of the west wing. I found this confusing—but not as much as when we continued descending even past the ground floor. Weren't we going to the bath? Was there even a basement in the beta…? But the knight's pace was utterly confident.

The stairs ended on the basement level, turning into a tiled-floor hallway lit by oddly colored lamps. As we walked, the chilly air gradually grew warmer and warmer.

Eventually, there was a large door on the right-hand wall. It wasn't adorned with a hanging curtain with the word for bath on it, like in Japan, but the open doorway was exuding white steam, so it was definitely the right place. In the real world, a place that steamy underground would get as moldy as you could possibly imagine, but we didn't have to worry about microorganisms or viruses in the virtual world—I hoped.

When Kizmel and Asuna passed through the door, I stopped and called out, "Okay, I'll wait for you here."

The knight swung around and beckoned to me, looking hurt. "Don't be silly, Kirito. Come in with us."

"Um…I'd feel bad if I forced you two to wear swimsuits like at Yofel Castle…Plus, on the one-in-a-million chance that those vagabonds attack again…"

Asuna looked exquisitely conflicted, trapped between her guilt at being the only one bathing and her desire to bathe properly in the buff, but Kizmel had no hesitation whatsoever.

"Do not worry about an attack," she said. "This castle can only be entered through the gate to the south, and when it opens, the bells can be heard all throughout the castle. And you need not worry about the other matter."

"Huh…?"

"Here, come and see."

She grabbed my arm and yanked me through the doorway.

It was a kind of rest lounge, decorated all over with attractive, leafy plants and tables with rattan chairs on either side wall. There were also pitchers and glasses for water. There were no other dark elves here, probably because it was still early. There were also two rattan doors on the far wall that likely led to the bath. There was a circle on the left door and a square on the right.

"The bath in this castle is very large, so there are separate entrances for men and women. You will not need your 'swem-soots' here, Kirito and Asuna."

"Oh...th-that makes sense..." I said, relieved. In that case, I wasn't opposed to relaxing in a nice huge bath. I didn't have anything against baths.

"We will see you later, then." Kizmel grinned. She and Asuna vanished through the circle door, waving, so I pushed my way through the square entrance. As I expected, there was a changing room next. It seemed appropriate to the fantasy genre that in addition to wicker baskets for holding clothes, there were also armor hooks. But thanks to my art of Mystic Scribing, I could just hit the UNEQUIP ALL button to have my clothes spirited away into storage. After a quick check to make sure no one else was around, I removed the last piece, too.

Using the provided white towel for the minimal level of defense, I headed through the next door. The tiled hallway turned left, leading toward...

"Ooh..."

It was a fantastical enough sight to elicit a murmur from me. The space was a massive dome with a radius of probably thirty feet. The gently curved walls and ceiling were clearly carved straight from the bedrock, but that just accentuated the natural hot spring feel. There were niches in the walls at even intervals, containing lamps that provided soft light to the chamber.

Under the dome was milky liquid of an opal-white color, and something that looked like a thick vine hung directly from the middle of the ceiling all the way down to the water. This dome was probably located right beneath the open plaza on the surface, which would mean the vine was a root of the spirit tree.

I put the towel in my inventory and set foot on the first step of the bath, allowing the heat to fill me up to the top of my head. This time, it elicited a *"Fwaaa..."* from my mouth. It was too shallow to get my whole body in, though, so I headed toward the center, parting the lingering steam as I went.

Near the root, it was as deep as my waist, so I finally dunked down into the water.

Just then, the white steam in front of me gave way, revealing another figure at startling proximity. It was too deep for me to leap out of the way, so all I could do was stare.

In general, I was not a person with a lot of reliance on regulations, self-control, or personal rules—but even I had a few things I demanded of myself.

One was never to think *If only I had (not) done this or that.* It was important to understand the reason things happened to ensure I didn't repeat my mistakes, but I considered worrying about *Why did you say that*, or *If only I'd realized this*, or *If I'd just started my homework earlier* to be nothing more than a waste of my limited mental resources over time.

But even I, in this one instant, couldn't help but consider a whole cornucopia of possible actions that I'd failed to take:

If only I'd been satisfied with the edge of the bath. If only I'd realized why the huge bath was a dome. If only I'd more closely considered Kizmel's description: *There are separate entrances for men and women. If only...*

If only I'd instantly closed my eyes, turned around, and claimed *"I didn't see anything!"* maybe there would have been a different result.

But what I actually did was stare, dumbfounded, for about three whole seconds at the female player standing barely two feet away with all her equipment removed. My eyesight auto-aim kicked in, going first from the collarbone down to the pelvic bone submerged in the water, then back up, until I finally saw her face.

At this moment, there was only one other player in Castle Galey aside from me. So naturally, this person staring equally dumbfounded back at me was my partner of about a month, Miss Asuna the fencer.

*Wow...after all that trouble, we've beaten five floor bosses in a month. At this rate, we could be on the tenth floor by mid-January,* I thought, my mind grasping for anything other than the reality

I was facing: Asuna's neck, jaw, and then nose turning fiery red. When the color reached her hairline, she grunted "Nngh!" and raised her arm with a violent splash. Upon seeing her clenched fist, I thought, *Well, I suppose I've earned this one, fair and squa— No, no, no, wait!*

I couldn't accept that punch. This castle wasn't under the anti-criminal code. If level-19 Asuna hit me with a full-power punch while I was unarmored, she would do damage to my HP, and that would change her cursor color to orange. Normally, when we were out of town, she carefully adjusted her jabs to play nice, but the gloves were literally off now.

"W-wait, no!" I yelled, but the God of Fury before me could hear no human words.

"*Hnnngggg!*" she roared, and before she could unleash her fists, I took the one option that would avoid her being designated a criminal player.

I toppled forward, not backward, and folded my arms around her body, then pushed her into the water, sending up a glorious plume of hot water. We sank nearly three feet into the cloudy bath.

I clutched the struggling girl, who continued trying to scream even under the water. I wanted to yell "*You're going to turn orange!*" but the only sound that came out of my mouth was "*Bw uh-bubbu-ba-beww-bowah-glurble-gurlurgle!*"

Naturally, the Drowning icon showed up above our HP bars, and with the way the air was escaping our mouths, HP loss wasn't far off. We couldn't let ourselves die for such a pathetic reason, so I pulled us up enough for our heads to breach the surface, still holding Asuna. This would be my final chance to warn her about going orange...

Then a deluge of freezing-cold water poured onto us from above, literally cooling our heads. I froze in place, completely bewildered. It was Kizmel, who had no doubt come to the bath later due to the process of manual armor removal, looking down on us. "Well, well, aren't we friendly?" she commented.

Naturally, she had not a single piece of equipment on, but by this point, I didn't have any mental power left to reflect on it.

Later on, I was told that the spirit tree at Castle Galey was constantly sucking up the natural hot spring water through its roots to support its branches and leaves, occasionally becoming so quenched that it dripped like rain to form the pool at its base. The cold pool steadily seeped into the bedrock, and every hour or so, it poured into the underground spring like a waterfall.

It made a certain kind of sense—and also made no sense at all—but the point was, it saved us from a variety of potential troubles. Asuna's class temporarily changed from Fencer to God of Fury, but when she remembered that we weren't in a safe haven, she realized what my actions were meant to do. She cycled through five or six different facial expressions before she said, "I apologize for doing that" and went back to being human again.

I sank down to my shoulders and considered what to do now. The water itself was almost completely opaque, so if you stayed five feet apart, you couldn't see the other person's body whatsoever, but I didn't have the willpower to sit back and enjoy my bath, even under those circumstances. It seemed that I should just equip the swimsuit Asuna made for me on the fourth floor, but for some reason, she was just soaking in a daze without doing the same, so I felt a bit hesitant to open my window.

In the end, I decided that simply finding a way to peel off and get out of there was best, and I was scooting off to the side when Kizmel, who was soaking on the other side of Asuna from me, started speaking.

"You know, about those throwing picks…I think I may know a way to counteract the poison that seeps from them."

"Wha…?"

That was exactly what I'd been hoping to ask her about. I scooted several inches closer out of sheer fixation—until a hard stare from Asuna held me at bay.

"If those throwing picks are indeed fashioned from the spikes of the dragon Shmargor, then the story of the human hero Selm fighting the dragon should be useful to consult. As I recall, Selm gained the assistance of an elven sage and constructed a tool to stop the dragon's poison…"

"Ooh…and how do you create that item?" I asked, leaning forward again. This time, Asuna was paying attention to Kizmel, so I didn't attract her ire.

"Was the sage a dark elf or a forest elf?"

Kizmel replied to these questions with a short shrug. "I heard the story from my grandmother when I was a child. I'm afraid I don't recall the finer details. But I believe a dark elf storyteller would have a full and proper recollection of the story of Shmargor."

"S-storyteller? Where can we go to meet such a person?"

*Please, please, let it be somewhere on a floor we've already cleared out, relatively close to the main town!* I prayed. It was answered with surprising helpfulness.

"There is a storyteller in this very castle. But as a general rule, they are very old and spend most of the day sleeping, so you will need to visit the library around the middle of the day."

"Nice!"

I just barely held back from throwing in a "*Sweet!*" as well. It wasn't confirmed yet that we'd be able to craft an antidote, but even the possibility was welcome.

As for Asuna, she found her interest drawn to something else. She turned to face Kizmel, rippling the surface of the bath.

"I've never seen an elderly elf before…Are they youthful in appearance, too?"

"Our elders rarely venture outside the city; that is why. As for their appearances…Well, I find that a difficult question to answer."

"Oh. Of course. I'll just look forward to finding out in person."

"That is a good idea. I think I'll get out now. What about you two?" the knight asked. We looked at each other for the briefest of moments, then agreed that we were done, too. I turned around, still crouched, and headed for the men's dressing room—though it didn't make sense to me why you'd have separate dressing rooms that led into the same bath. But before I left, one last question crossed my mind, and I turned back around.

"Oh yeah, Kizmel—"

Into my line of sight leaped the upper half of the standing knight—and Asuna desperately using both hands to cover her up. I quickly averted my eyes.

"Hmm? What is it, Kirito?"

"Uh…I-I'll ask in the lounge! Um, s-see you later!"

I quickly beat a breaststroke retreat across the bath for the stairs before any further attacks could come my way.

One of the nice things about *SAO* was that wet hair and skin dried very quickly upon leaving the water. So I didn't need to towel off as I headed down the dark hallway to the changing room, equipped a black shirt and pants, and entered the lounge. The women weren't back yet, and no one else was visiting the place, so I slumped lazily into one of the rattan chairs along the wall and heaved a deep sigh.

I had no issues with bathing in general, but it had been the source of trouble more than once or twice since I partnered up with Asuna: I had to wear a skimpy suit with a bear logo on it in Yofel Castle, and there, I got my head dunked. I had to guard Asuna while she bathed at the dark elf camp on the third floor, where Kizmel barged in on me. Nothing much happened on the second floor, but on the first…

"Actually…I think bathing was the start of all this…" I muttered, pouring water from the pitcher on the table into a glass and drinking it all down.

As a matter of fact, when we first met, Asuna hadn't removed her red riding hood for anyone, and the moment when it first felt like the distance between us was closing the tiniest bit was when she came to the place I'd been renting out in Tolbana on the first floor of Aincrad. Her visit was to use my bath.

With exquisitely poor timing, Argo the info dealer arrived

while she was bathing, having run across her while trying to slip into the bathroom to change equipment. But if I hadn't been renting out a place with a deluxe bath in the first place, we might not have ever found ourselves working together.

So no matter how many times it led to incidents, I couldn't hold ill will against the baths of Aincrad…I just needed to make sure I knew the men's and women's baths were fully separate next time.

The swinging door with the circle mark on it opened, and Asuna and Kizmel returned. The fencer was wearing a yellow tunic I'd never seen before, while the knight was in a shimmering purple gown—both noticeably more sheer than their usual clothes, which flustered me at first (even though it seemed unnecessary to get worked up about, after what had just happened in the bath).

Fortunately, Asuna's memories of that disaster had been overwritten by the pleasure of her first Aincrad bath in a natural hot spring. She threw herself into the rattan chair on my right, a look of bliss on her face, and said, "Ahhh…that was good…"

I handed her a cup of cold water, which she gulped down. *"Pweeh!"*

Kizmel sat in the chair on my left, elegantly folding her long legs, and said, "It is indeed quite a splendid bath we have here. It is a shame I will have to move again, once my duty on this floor is over."

"I see. You've got a busy life, Kizmel…You've got the, um…Jade and Lapis and Amber Keys stored in a safe location, right?"

"But of course. They are in the treasure repository on the fourth floor of the central hall."

"T-treasure repository, huh…?"

*I'd sure like to see that. But I bet it's the type of place where I'll get yelled at*, I wondered selfishly, but Asuna had a much more practical thought in mind:

"Kizmel…aren't you worried that the forest elves might attack in search of the keys again, like they did at Yofel Castle?"

This was a very good question. Thick stone walls and massive gate aside, this place would make a significantly easier target than Yofel Castle, which was surrounded by water on all sides. The forest elves had put so much effort into seizing the keys back, it was hard to imagine them giving up after one defeat.

There could be enemy soldiers sneaking up outside the gates even as we sat here. The disquieting thought nearly got me up out of my seat.

"...No. You need not worry about that," Kizmel stated. Both Asuna and I stared at the side of her face. Something in the faint gloom of her expression told me the source of her certainty.

"Oh, I see. The area outside this castle..."

"That's right. The wasteland that surrounds us is so desolate and dry...that neither dark elf nor forest elf can last within it for long. Inside the castle, we are protected by the blessings of the spirit tree, but if that tree was to die out, we would be forced to abandon this place."

When I visited Castle Galey in the beta, the dark elf who gave me the quest—neither Kizmel nor Count Galeyon, just a nameless commander—told me the same thing. I took it at face value at the time, but now it only brought fresh questions.

"But then, how will you get the key on this floor back? You can telep...er, travel through the spirit trees at the castles on the fifth and seventh floor, but the key is still far from this place, isn't it?"

"That's correct," she admitted. There still seemed to be a faint note of mourning on her features, but when she turned to us, she was wearing her usual languid smile. "But do not fear. This castle is equipped with a means to leave in the case of a sudden emergency. It will allow us to cross the arid wastes."

At that, my partner and I shared a meaningful look. We didn't need to speak aloud to understand each other.

"Kizmel," Asuna said, "Kirito and I will retrieve the hidden key on this floor. We might not be as strong as you, but we're much tougher than we used to be."

"I do not doubt that," the elf replied, looking hesitant, "but I cannot expect you to do the job for me. The friction with the forest and

Fallen Elves is our problem…And think of it this way. If you had not saved my life in the Forest of Wavering Mists, I would have been killed by that forest elf—or we would have fought to our mutual deaths, at best. How can I be allowed to stay safe and sound in a castle while allowing you two to do all the dirty, dangerous work?"

*"Just like this, that's how!"* I wanted to shout, but the look on the proud knight's face prevented me. Asuna appeared to have more to say on the matter, but I waved her back and said, "All right… then let's go and get the key tomorrow. But don't take unnecessary risks. If any of it seems tough, you must promise to tell us at once."

I held out my left pinkie finger, which Kizmel stared at.

"What is wrong with your finger?"

"Oh, uh…It's a human custom. When you make a promise, you intertwine your pinkies."

"Ah. Like this?"

Kizmel hooked her right pinkie around mine and moved her hand up and down. Asuna got up from her chair saying "Me too!" and held out her right hand to Kizmel, who used her free hand to do the same, smiling awkwardly.

"It is a strange custom, but it feels fun. I promise not to take unnecessary risks, if you promise to prioritize your own safety."

"Of course!" Asuna and I replied in unison. The knight beamed.

After the underground bath, she led us to the dining room on the second floor of the central hall.

It was dinnertime, and many elves were present. There was even a small stage, upon which two elves in fanciful costumes were playing a lute and flute. Some of the soldiers were even singing quietly along to the tune.

The food itself was noticeably simpler than the full-course meal at Yofel Castle, but this way suited my taste better, and the stew of tubers and meat on the bone was good enough that I asked for seconds.

After deciding when we'd meet in the morning, we said good-bye to Kizmel at the third-floor hallway of the west wing—even though the knight's room was just next to ours—and returned to our guest chamber. We let out heavy breaths and found ourselves glancing at each other.

It felt like I needed to apologize for my scandalous behavior in the bath, but Asuna was sending a silent signal for me not to say anything at all. My game window said it wasn't even eight o'clock yet, which, on a typical day, meant I'd head back out for some night activity, but we were tired from the dungeon spelunking and crossing the wasteland today and agreed that we should get an early bedtime.

But we failed to realize that we hadn't yet faced the greatest peril of the day.

This guest chamber was another suite, where the living room was located in a separate area from the sleeping area. But unlike the place we stayed the night before, there was only one bedroom door.

We looked at each other again, then crossed the living room and opened the door. The bedroom was equally decadent, but there was just one queen-sized bed in the center of the room.

Last night, I'd slept on the sofa rather than my bed, so I could just do the same thing—except that was because Asuna had fallen fast asleep first. Knowing how my partner hated to be given special treatment, I suspected...

"Um...I'll just sleep on the sofa, okay...?"

"You're not going to get a good night's sleep that way."

I would've protested, but she was actually right, and she knew it.

While sleeping in *SAO*, the player's real-life body was in a sleep state as well, but the NerveGear kept faithfully sending virtual bodily signals all the while. If you slept on a fancy bed, you would feel the softness envelop your back. If you slept outdoors on the ground, it would be rough and uncomfortable. Naturally, the latter would provide shallower sleep, often failing to result in anything more than a surface-level snooze.

The sofa in the living room was large enough, and its mattress was nice and thick, but because the seat cushions were mounded, it wasn't suitable for lying down on. When I was soloing on the first floor, I camped out all the time—with a blanket, at least—so I could sleep on this, but whether Asuna accepted that or not was a different matter.

"Listen, I can sleep anywhere. Don't mind me, just take the bed and—"

"We *are* game partners, aren't we?" Asuna interrupted.

She was correct, of course.

"Y-yeah?"

"So it would be wrong to place all the burden on one of us."

Again, she was absolutely correct.

"...Y-yeah."

"Then this is the only option."

She dragged me by the sleeve into the bedroom and peeled back half the covers on the large bed. Right in the center of the perfectly pristine white sheets, she drew a line two feet long down the middle with her finger.

"This is the border."

I hadn't heard that word since the time we slept in Kizmel's tent in the dark elf camp on the third floor, and the surprise brought a burst of laughter to my lips—and a fierce glare from Asuna.

"A-all right...I get it. I understand. Capisce."

Asuna gave me a scowl back, but she indicated this was sufficient and put the covers back.

While we'd landed on a compromise for the bed issue, the circumstances were a little—no, a lot—different from the tent. Sleeping on the ground there meant excusing a lot of potential contact under the general experience of "roughing it." But in a proper building, a proper bedroom, a proper bed, there could be no excuses. The border drawn on the sheets was as fragile and perilous as the Line of Control in Kashmir.

But for being so susceptible to spontaneous accidents, the fencer exhibited surprising fortitude toward this situation.

"Well...I'll sleep on this side," she said, taking the half farther away from the window and slipping under the blanket. With her back to me, she opened her window, pressed a button or two, then closed it. I heard a swishing sound under the covers, which was probably her changing into pajamas.

Then she wriggled down deeper until only the back of her head was visible. It seemed her strategy was to fall asleep as soon as possible, which seemed like the right call to me, so I tapped the wall and turned off the lights in the bedroom and living room.

There was a window on the west bedroom wall, and gauzy moonlight trickled through the lace curtains. The day started off cloudy but cleared up in the afternoon. *Hopefully the weather will be nice tomorrow,* I thought, trying to distract myself as I entered the side of the bed opposite Asuna.

The bed was about six feet across, so as long as I stayed on the very left edge, far from the border, I didn't need to be conscious of my partner's presence, physically speaking. Whatever the mattress was made of, it had just the right mixture of support and softness, and the blanket was light and as warm as a down comforter. I had to admit that Asuna was right; the sofa out there and my heavy-duty camping blanket were a far cry from this kind of comfort.

My head sank into the massive pillow, and my eyelids closed, and despite the situation, I felt the sleep fairy sneaking up on me. *There we go—fall asleep, fall asleep, and get an extra room tomorrow...*

"Are you still awake, Kirito?"

"………Ayup."

The fairy had scampered away. If she said "*Just checking,*" what kind of a snappy response should I have? But the follow-up from over the border was not what I was expecting.

"You know how there's that anti-harassment code? The thing that came up in Mr. Romolo's workshop on the fourth floor when you tried to wake me up?"

"Y…yes."

This ominous topic dispelled my sleepiness entirely. Now I had no idea where she was taking this.

"I was just thinking…you pushed me over when we were in the bath."

"N-no…I was keeping you from going orange."

"But you pushed me over."

"………Ayup."

"So why didn't the anti-harassment code activate?"

*Why didn't it…?*

I didn't have an answer on the tip of my tongue. I had to think about it.

"Um…Does it not show up if you're in a party together…? No, because we were partied up on the fourth floor…Maybe it depends on the time of contact…? But no, I don't remember touching you for very long on the fourth floor, either…"

"It's not an issue of how you make contact. When you tried to wake me up, you just touched my shoulder, and it went off, but it didn't happen when you pushed me over naked."

"P-please don't say it like that…" I begged.

Indeed, it wasn't logical that the code activated just from touching her shoulder, and yet, pressing against her without any equipment on didn't do a thing. Was there any other condition that was different between the workshop and the underground hot spring, aside from party configuration and time of contact?

"Mmm-hmmmm…"

I chased away the sleep fairy, who was trying to sneak back into my mind. But the soft, fluffy bed was just so soft and fluffy, and if it was any softer and fluffier, it would soft…fluff…

"……Ah."

The instant I began tumbling off the precipice into sleep was the hint I needed.

"When it happened…you were sleeping."

She must have been nodding off, too, because her reply came at a delay.

"…What? The code activated because I was sleeping? You mean it won't go off if you're awake…?"

"…No, I don't think that's it…But that's the only thing I can think of…"

"Hmm……"

After another silence of many seconds, my temporary partner surprised me once more.

"Pinkie..."

"Eh?"

"Hold out your pinkie."

I wriggled my little finger through the blanket, then remembered the invisible line.

"But the border—"

"One finger's worth of trespassing can be overlooked. Hurry it up."

"Okay..."

Hesitantly, I stretched my arm, sticking out my pinkie near the centerline of the bed. After a few moments, what I assumed was Asuna's pinkie brushed mine and grabbed it. On instinct, I squeezed back.

"So, um...what are we doing?"

"Just be quiet."

"......"

"...The window for the code isn't popping up. So if we fall asleep like this, and it's showing when we wake up, that would indicate that your theory is correct, to a degree."

"......Ah, I see..."

The tension drained out of my body. Asuna's pinkie pressure eased a little bit, and she whispered, "Well, good night..."

"If the prompt does show up, don't hit the button in your sleep."

"Yeah...I...know..."

"Good night."

From that point on, silence fell on the land of the blankets, and the only thing coming over the border was the faint sound of sleeping. I closed my eyes again, but the gentle warmth of that pinkie contact prevented my wits from dispersing to all corners.

I was curious about the workings of the anti-harassment code, of course, but there were still many things for Asuna and me to do on this floor yet. We hadn't finished the "Curse of Stachion" quest, we had to help advance progress through the floor, the

handling of the guild flag was still up in the air, and tomorrow, we'd be helping Kizmel with the quest to retrieve the Agate Key. And the biggest problem of all was the PKers.

I'd told myself on numerous occasions that it was pointless trying to decipher their way of thinking, but I still couldn't help myself.

Why were Morte, the dagger user, and the man in the black poncho trying to make the DKB and ALS fight? Especially when it was obvious that it would only harm our chances of beating this game and finding freedom from its electronic prison?

No matter their reasons, I would never forgive them for the act of attempting to kill Asuna. I would never let their wicked blades anywhere near her again.

For an instant, I was seized by a shockingly powerful urge.

I didn't want this pinkie.

I wanted to grab her hand, pull her close, and wrap my arms around her. I wanted to make it clear that I was going to keep her safe.

But I couldn't do that. Our partnership probably wasn't going to last forever, and it shouldn't. Until the day she stood at the lead of our best and brightest, standing as a symbol of hope for all the players of the game, I would continue providing her with whatever help I could, as a beta tester. That was my role.

I let the tension slowly drain out of my body, exhaled, and tensed my finger one more time, just to feel that the sensation was still there.

...*Good night*, I whispered in my mind, and I gave myself up to sleep at last.

*(To be continued)*

# AFTERWORD

Thank you for reading *Sword Art Online Progressive 5*, "Canon of the Golden Rule (Start)."

The previous volume originally came out in December 2015, which means it's been over two years since we left off. I'm very sorry about that. I'm also very sorry that this is the first two-part story in this series!

*SAOP* has been proceeding at the pace of one floor per volume, but even then, each volume required some part of the story to be told in digest form (quests, advancing through the floor, boss fights), and I always regretted that…So I decided that I wanted to write as much of this floor as possible this time around. But once I started, I realized there was too much to contain to one book, especially with lots of Kizmel material, and the idea of cutting anything after all that was too much to bear. So I've decided to make this a two-volume story and get it all out of my system. Because of that, all kinds of things are left hanging at the end of this book, but the second half should be coming very soon after this, so please, just have a bit of patience for our arrival at the seventh floor! Please!

As for the content…I chose to make the theme of the sixth floor "puzzles" because I always wanted to do a puzzle-based floor, but I'm also not very good at solving puzzles in dungeons whenever they show up in RPGs (*laughs*). Especially in MMOs—when it requires the coordination of several players at once. I feel like I'm getting an ulcer imagining myself being the one who screwed up and got yelled at by everyone else. I plan to put Kirito in just such a tricky situation in the second half, so let's all cheer him on and hope he gets it right the first time!

Some of you might also be worried about how fast Kirito and Asuna seem to be getting closer by the volume. So am I! The idea is for the *Progressive* series to connect to the main series, so having them be so hunky-dory in the early stages feels like it's straining the space-time continuum, but I will continue my irresponsible policy of leaving it all up to them and trusting it'll *probably* work itself out in the end.

I also have a few announcements…At about the same time as this book, the *Fatal Bullet* game should be coming out. It's set in the world of *GGO*, and it's the first major release that features an original protagonist, so I hope you enjoy adventuring alongside Kirito and Asuna. Also, the mobile game *Integral Factor* is an MMORPG about conquering Aincrad from the very first floor, just like *Progressive*, so you should definitely check it out!

Lastly, to my illustrator, abec, and my editors, Miki and Adachi, my deepest apologies and thanks for putting up with my edge-of-your-seat deadline completion! I hope I see the rest of you in the second half of this book, coming soon!

*Reki Kawahara—December 2017*